For all those that didn't believe in me

To my Nan Patricia, for being my proof reader

To Lois for also being my proof reader

To Sam, for all the hours spent editing

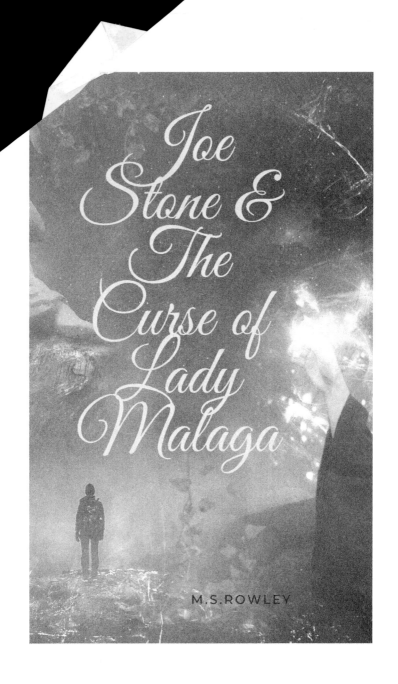

Joe Stone & The Curse of Lady Malaga

M.S.ROWLEY

Contents

Chapter 1

THE WEATHER

On a cold and wet windy morning, you could hear the howling, screeching wind rattling through the front door letter box, through the cracks in the bathroom window, and through the old floor boards. This had been the same for the last five days, the weather seemed like it was getting worse by the day. The rubbish bins had been flung down the road like they weighed nothing, birds battling to stay in the sky but losing the fight to fly, this wasn't what you would expect to happen on a normal day. When you thought nothing else could happen, it did.

It was mid morning when it happened, suddenly there was a flash of bright light across the sky, it covered all the houses upon all of the streets. It was so bright that is caused all of the neighbours to run out of the safety of their homes to see this strange but beautiful light. It was so bright you couldn't even look at it. In the time it had taken the light to appear, it had vanished and the weather was back to its normal wet and windy self. It was that bad people were running back inside their homes. What was happening?

This weather continued for at least two hours, all I was thinking was how beautiful that beam of light was, what was it and where did it go. A shrill ring pierced the quietness of the house and Mum rushed to the phone, a few minutes later, the phone dropped from Mum's hand, her face had turned an ashen white like she had seen a ghost. She turned to face me and said 'Oh no.'

'What is it,' I replied.

'It's happening' Mum said.

None of this made sense and I was getting more confused as time went on.

'You need to pack a bag now, quick.'

By the time I had finished throwing some clothes into a bag, I was in a state of bewilderment with what was happening. One minute the weather was cold and wet, then the sky was filled with a beam of light, Mum started to scream at me to pack a bag. I was hoping all this was just a dream and that I would wake up and everything would be as it was on any other day.

I could feel the adrenaline surging through my body as I didn't know what was going on. We ran to the car and chucked our bags in the boot, Mum closed the boot with a slam and we both got in the car. Mum couldn't wait to get on the road, the car was filled with the smell of burning rubber as Mum pulled away. Through the window I saw an old lady looking very sad with tears in her eyes waving us goodbye, there was a faint dark figure behind the old lady, my eyes must have been playing tricks on me. A few minutes later, Mum had started to calm down.

'I'm sorry if I scared you son, there is something that I need to tell you but the time isn't right just yet. I didn't mean to panic you but we needed to get away fast.'

My heart was beating so fast I could feel it coming through my chest. Looking out the window objects just flashed past, that's how fast Mum was driving, a few times during the journey I kept closing my eyes to try and make sense of what was happening.

'I will explain everything I promise, but first we need to get to Uncle Barry's. We will tell you everything, just lie back and fall asleep, I will wake you when we get there.'

Uncle Barry lives a few hours away from us, so I lay back and fell asleep. I close my eyes and begin to drift off thinking of nice things. I must have fallen asleep for what felt like thirty minutes, then woke up suddenly with Mum shaking my arm. 'Wake up, we have arrived.'

That couldn't have been two hours that I was asleep, but it must have been. As I looked out of the window, we were making our way up a very long driveway that lead up to a big mansion of a house. Beautiful green trees lined the driveway and the house had big beautiful gold stained glass windows. I've never been here before, I'd only ever seen photos of Uncle Barry standing outside this house. He is a very private person and did not like to see or meet with anyone else.

Mum pulled up outside the front of the house and Uncle Barry was waiting to meet us with his arms outstretched. As the car came to a stop, I ran out of the car and into my Uncle's arms, this felt odd, as I had never met this man. I looked up at the amazingly built house and couldn't wait to explore and see what secrets this house held.

'Come on, lets get the stuff out of the boot,' said Mum

'Come in come in, it's so lovely to see you both,' Uncle Barry replied.

I just knew that Uncle Barry was putting on an act as he had the same look on his face that my Mum did. I knew this house and Uncle Barry held all the secrets of the bright beam of light this morning. They knew the time had come to reveal the secrets they had been entrusted to keep.

This is where our story begins, I am Joe and my Mum is called Stella and you know who Uncle Barry is. We have lived in our small village called Garden View since before I could remember. I'm guessing our village gained its name because all you can see are row upon row of gardens. The neighbours are all very friendly and they are on hand should we ever need any help. I am just a normal kid who loves playing video games or going out with my friends, to my knowledge we were a normal family. My Dad was never at home, he was always away working, I didn't ask too much, Mum just said he's working and that was that. Mum rang Dad every night without fail, to see how he was getting on. There was an old lady next door but didn't really see much of her. Mum would always ask to see if she would like anything from the our local shop, but she knew if she needed anything Mum would get it for her. Living a few doors down was a girl called Becky, but she preferred to be called Bex. We would meet up a few times a week but her parents were very strict with her and limited the time we could spend with each other. We both go to the same school, our school was called Garden View High, it was ok, the school wasn't too big and the teachers were nice. I didn't really like school much, I just wanted to be at home helping my Mum and playing on my games. My greatest wish would be that something would change and I could have the greatest adventure.

'Joe.' Shouted Uncle Barry pulling me out of my day dream.

'Yes Uncle Barry' I replied back.

'Follow me and I will show you your room whilst staying at my house, bring your bags with you.'

I followed Barry up wide long staircases that seemed to go on for ever. I was amazed at seeing all the pictures hanging on the wall and lights dropping down from the celling. I had never seen anything like it before. Mum was pacing along the hallway at the top of the stairs. How did she get up here before us I wondered as we reached the hallway, she turned and looked directly at me and said,

'Joe, I know what is happening right now must be very strange and will have you wondering what is going on but I will explain everything and Uncle Barry will help me out. Now is the right time you were told, I will make us some tea and we can all sit down and start explaining.'

I didn't know if I wanted to know or if everything should have been kept a secret from me but I did not have a choice in what was about to happen. We made our way downstairs to the drawing room and sat on a large sofa with steaming cups of tea Mum had made. The cups were made from the most beautiful gold I had ever seen. I was amazed that everything Uncle Barry had was made from this gold from the windows down to the tea cups. What did my Uncle do to afford this luxurious lifestyle.

'Stella' Uncle Barry shouts in a soft calm voice,

'Yes Barry' replies my Mum,

'I think it's time that young Joe knows the truth, don't you?'

Mums hands started to shake and she was trying her best not to drop her tea all over Uncle Barry's cream rug.

'Yes it is Barry, can you do the explaining.'

'Of course.'

Uncle Barry turns to me and says 'Joe you're a very special boy, we have all been trying to keep you safe, even your Dad. He's not been working, he's been hunting down a lady, that is very dangerous to us all. She has tried to hurt a lot of people, she's a witch Joe.'

My mouth dropped open and my head started to spin with confusion. This couldn't be true could it. I knew I wanted an adventure but this was all getting a bit too much to handle right now. I turned to look at my Uncle Barry and started to laugh nervously.

'You're joking right?'

'No my boy I'm not, this is no laughing matter. She is very dangerous she's back, that beam of light that was her, that's why you're here Joe.'

I let my head fall back into the sofa and felt an odd sense of calm wash over me. I felt all warm and cozy all of a sudden. Uncle Barry turned to my Mum and said 'It's time now, he's ready to see the whole truth.'

All of a sudden the calm I had felt a few moments before left my body and I was shocked to be hearing what was being said. With all the energy I had left, I said 'The whole truth what does that even mean?'

'You will see Uncle Barry said.'

All of a sudden the cup of tea I had suddenly started to swirl and change colour to red.

'Don't be scared now boy, I see you have just seen your tea. I need you to drink that, it will feel strange at first, but the tea lets you see back into the past and you will see how this all started.'

I just stared at Barry and without warning, he grabs my cup off the coffee table and passed it to me.

'Drink up now and you will see the truth you need to see.'

I took the cup off Uncle Barry, I was scared to drink it because of what I might see, but I knew I was in safe hands.

'Uncle Barry, why do I feel all warm and have no energy?'

'The tea you have drank so far makes your body ready for the next stage. This is why it has gone red this is telling you that you need to drink it now. Your body is in a relaxed state ready for you to see the past.'

I lifted the cup up to my mouth and felt the red tea pass my lips. It was slightly cold but had a tingling feeling. I could feel it running through my body and my eyes were starting to close and all I could see was red. 'Wait' I shouted out.

'I can see a door,'

'Yes that's it, walk on through it.' Uncle Barry replied.

I started to panic with what was happening, where was I and what was this place, I had a feeling my life would not be the same again.

Chapter 2

THE PAST

I was walking through a small village town, I could see nobody around at all apart from a lady sitting in the middle of the town square's fountain, crying her eyes out and making loud sobs. All I could hear was her saying that someone had taken her mother. She suddenly screamed out and I walked towards her.

'It's ok, don't cry.' I said to her.

She didn't acknowledge that I had said anything, it was like I wasn't even there. I then realised that I was visiting the past and remembered that I would be able to see people but they would not be able to see me. I needed to find out what was going on. The woman got up from the fountain edge and I started to follow. As I walked behind her I noticed her long white hair snaking its way down her back and a long white gown that looked almost angelic, was I really looking at an angel? I was trying to keep up with her as she continued to walk up a village road. All of a sudden and out of nowhere a man come up and grabbed hold of her.

I heard him shout at her, where is the book of evil, he said if she didn't tell him, that her mother would not have long to live. She fought back against him and pushed him away and replied 'please don't hurt my Mum.' He began to walk away laughing and I could tell that he wasn't pleased with this strange but angelic woman. I knew I needed to help this woman and find out what was happening, why this man had taken her Mum and what the hell was the book of evil. All of sudden the town I was in began to melt away and the scene I was watching began to change.

I was now in a dark, dank house with only a spare candlelight burning and lighting the room I was in. The lady I was following was sat in the corner of the room, one minute I was in the town following her and now I was in her house, well a low beamed ceiling cottage if I was honest. In the middle of the room and barely lit was something on a tall shelf and the only way I could see it was because of the candle light glinting on the shiny exterior. What was this shiny object and what was this woman doing. She took the object and it changed to become a big book, I could have sworn it did not look like a book a minute ago. It must have changed itself to disguise what it truly was.

I could hear her mutter at the book, 'there you are my friend' whilst gripping the book so tight that I could see her hands and knuckles turn white. She started to caress the book's cover and say 'I need you to help my mother, your contents are the only thing that will be able to save her.'

Once again the scene started to change and I was starting to feel a little dizzy and sick with all the changing. I looked around as the new place came into view. I was back in the town square with the fountain's water making a beautiful trickling sound. All of a sudden horrendous screams and shouts filled the town square, within seconds people were coming from every direction and gathering together. With all the commotion all I could make out was people shouting for a witch to be killed. Out of one of the biggest buildings to the side of the town square an elderly woman was dragged and tied to a big bit of wood next to the fountain. She looked so helpless with tears running down her face. She had her eyes looking right on me and I had my eyes on her. Suddenly she turned her head to the left and was looking upon the angelic woman from earlier on, you could tell that this was mother and daughter, I could barely make out what she said, 'it's ok my dear, I love you so very much.' All of a sudden there was a burst of light and I felt like I was falling, I opened my eyes and I was back in my Uncle Barry's house.

'Uncle Barry. I haven't seen everything that was happening.'

'The tea can only show you so much of what was happening and not everything.'

I was so disappointed with only being shown a little bit of what was happening, I had truly thought that my adventure was just beginning and now I was back here. I wanted to see more. My Mum came over and wrapped her arms around me and said 'This is only the start of what happened, the woman you saw after you drank the tea isn't very nice at all'

'She seemed so nice and almost angelic and was only trying to help her Mum, I would do the same for you Mum.'

'She was indeed Joe, but she couldn't help her, she was too late. She now seeks revenge.'

'But why us?'

"That is enough for one night Joe, I want you to go up stairs and get ready for bed'.

'But Mum.'

'Now please.'

I have just been told things that will change my life and my Mum wants me to go bed, I won't be able to get this out of my head at all. From what I saw, she seemed so nice and why would she want revenge. I walked up the stairs and waited on the hallway for my Mum and Uncle Barry to start talking. I could hear Uncle Barry say 'I think Joe took that well' and I could just picture the big grin on his face. My Mum replied saying 'I hope you know what you're doing Barry, I do not want my son coming to any harm.' I began walking towards my room and heard Uncle Barry say everything was under control and that he will be showing me more tomorrow so that I knew what I would be facing. I could picture my mum putting her head into her hands and shaking side to side, she did this all the time when she was angry with me.

I continued to listen to the conversation between my Mum and Uncle Barry.

"Don't worry he will be fine, we both knew this day would come, and we can't hide him away any longer. Right I'm off to bed myself, I'll see you in the morning, get plenty of sleep we are going to need it.'

'Goodnight Barry.'

'Are you not going yourself?'

'I will be soon, I just have to make a phone call.'

I can hear my Mum pacing up and down grabbing her phone and calling my Dad.

'It's done, he knows.'

'Thats good news, we now can show him what he needs to know' replied my dad.

'Are you coming home soon? We all need you so much right now.'

'It won't be long, we may have found the location of you know who.'

'Really?, please be careful.'

'You know that she will be after Joe, keep him safe i'll be back soon, love you.'

'Love you too good night.'

I ran as quietly as I could, down the hallway to my room and collapsed onto my bed, exhaustion had taken over my body and I fell into a restless sleep. I woke up to the smell of breakfast that my Mum was cooking down in the kitchen and my stomach grumbled in hunger. I was shocked to find that I had fallen asleep on top of the bed still in the same clothes from last night. I heard Mum shouting up the stairs that my breakfast was ready and I called back to her that I was just getting ready and that I would be down. I quickly got ready and raced down the stairs. I was a lot more hungry than I thought and didn't know what had caused this sudden hunger as I didn't eat much breakfast.

'Do you want a cup of tea Joe' Mum says with a grin on her face.

I started to laugh and replied 'Not one that's red.'

Mum looked round at me and started to laugh put a pot of tea on the table for me to help myself. Mum started making me some eggs.

'How do you want your eggs Joe, fried, boiled or scrambled?'

Before I could even say anything, Uncle Barry shouts over towards my Mum and told her to stop fussing over me.

I was very shocked by his response, it's almost like he had changed over night, he pulled out the kitchen chair and slammed his tea on the table, and gave me an evil stare.

'Whats wrong?' I asked with no reply.

'Joe, Joe' Mum says.

'Come here now.'

I went to my Mum and she whispered into my ear, Barry can be like this sometimes. It's best to just leave him to it, he will be ok in a minute. He doesn't like mornings, now here take your breakfast. I took my breakfast and started to eat without giving Uncle

Barry any eye contact. My Mum's scrambled eggs on toast slathered in butter was the best. I took a big gulp of my tea and then went back to my toast. All of a sudden Uncle Barry shouted 'right' and I almost jumped out of my chair as I wasn't expected anything from Uncle Barry.

'You ready then boy?' snarled Uncle Barry

'Ready for what?'

'The next part of learning the truth.'

I began questioning myself if I was ready to learn more of the truth, I didn't know why I was asking myself this silly question, I already knew the answer… Hell Yes!

'Yes please Uncle Barry' I answered quietly

'Well don't just sit there, come with me.'

I looked over at Mum and she had a nervous smile on her face and gave me a slight nod and I knew that I had to follow him. Off you go now said my Mum and I quickly hurried after Uncle Barry. I followed Uncle Barry as he lead the way past the front room and out into the garden. On the other side of the garden stood a big outer building sealed shut with two large wooden doors. Uncle Barry unlocked the doors and pushed them open and my mouth dropped open in amazement. It was like something out of this world, the ceiling and walls were all gold and down one wall there were lots of golden shelves filled with all manner of weird and wonderful things. My eyes caught on to something I instantly recognised, it can't be can it… It was the shiny object from yesterday that I saw when I was in the past. I turned to Uncle Barry as he knew that I had sen the book.

'Yes my boy, that is the book' said Uncle Barry

'What, how and why is it here?'

At that point I knew this wasn't good news that the book was here. Uncle Barry made me promise that I would not tell my Mum that the book was there, I knew I didn't have a choice as he looked so angry when I had seen the book.

'Good lad, now lets get started shall we?'

What does he mean, does my Mum know him as well as she thought she did, so much was running through my mind but I have to let that go for now and do what I was told.

Barry walked over to the book and picked it up, it started to get brighter as he walked towards me, then all of a sudden there was the same beam of light I had seen yesterday at home.

'Now boy we need to open this up but when we do it can be very dangerous.'

I didn't know what I was meant to do, did I follow what Uncle Barry was telling me to do or did I run and get my Mum. I guessed that I should just follow instructions for now. I gripped onto the book as Uncle Barry passed it over to me and I noticed how heavy it was.

'Be careful now boy.' He was standing there looking at me with an evil stare in his eye.

'Well, don't just look at the book open it right now' shouted Uncle Barry.

I was now starting to worry as I didn't think Uncle Barry was ok, with a tight grip on the book I flipped open the front cover and suddenly there was a shot of light that thrust upwards out of the book and hit the ceiling, it started to get heavier and heavier and I could not hold it any longer. Uncle Barry's face started to change and a loud laugh started to echo throughout the room after escaping from within Uncle Barry.

'You silly boy' choked out Uncle Barry amongst the laughs

Suddenly I knew this was not Uncle Barry, this was someone else and I had a sneaking feeling I knew who it was. It was the woman from the past that I saw yesterday but this time she was wearing a long black dress decorated with lacing black patterns throughout. Her hair flowed freely down her back and this was also a black colour. Suddenly and unexpectedly the shot of light filled the whole room and then she was gone along with the book that I was holding.

I could see my Mum and Uncle Barry running towards me, Uncle Barry shouted at me asking what I had done.

'I thought it was you Uncle.'

'She's now got the book and she's tricked you boy'

'It's not your fault Joe you didn't know.' Mum said as she wrapped her arms around me in a hug.

'Barry make Joe a cup of tea now, make him the blue mixture, we need to let Joe see everything now.'

Barry ran across the garden and into the house and presumably started to make the blue tea, that I would soon be drinking. I needed to know everything in this weird and wonderful adventure I was finding myself in.

We made our way across the garden and into the front room, I sat down on the sofa and again felt myself sink into a peaceful state of mind. Uncle

Barry came back into the front room with a cup full of blue tea and handed it to me. Without any hesitation, I drank the whole cup and started to feel the warmth of the tea work it's way through my body. I closed my eyes and suddenly felt this intense heat. What was happening, all I could see was flames and hear a lady shouting, I knew I had returned to the same place as yesterday. The heat I was feeling stopped and so had the shouting of the woman.

I heard a different woman say that she was sorry and that she had let her Mum down but not to worry as the people who had done this will pay. She sat in the town square and the white dress that she was wearing started to change gradually into a dusty black colour. Gone was the flowing white hair she had yesterday and in its place was a dirty black colour. She shouted across the town that she cursed everyone because of all the hatred they had caused. She turned to a man and screamed that this was all his fault and that he would pay not with his death but with eternal life. Forever watching his loved ones and family die.

You could feel the hatred coming off her in waves and this seemed to infect everything from the people around her to the trees lining the village. She was holding the book I had seen in her house yesterday and this morning in Uncle Barry's house. She opened the book and started muttering a language I had never heard. I knew this was a magic spell, as she spoke a feeling fell over the village, you could only describe as evil. This did not feel good and I knew this was a curse. As she cast her curse, the trees leaves turned from a lush green to a dark dingy brown and fell to the ground. The man she had cursed a moment ago shouted for her to stop but it was too late. She turned to look at the man and she looked so very scary. Her face had changed to a dark shade of blue black and from this angle I saw how truly evil a person could become. She was so upset about her mother and no one in her way could stop her. The rage she had was so powerful, I don't think she recognised herself anymore. She started to laugh and said in a voice that chilled me to the bone that everyone will be very sorry. She then thrust her hands out in front of her and a flash of green light fired between her and the man. I shouted out in shock for the man to watch out and forgot that they could not see or hear me.

By the time I had shouted out it was too late, the green light hit the man squarely in the chest and changed shape to form a green cage that he could not escape from. She laughed as she accomplished what she had set out to do and moved up through the town. People were rushing out of their homes to see what was happening. I shouted out again for people not to come out of their homes and for those who had to get back inside. This time she must have seen me as she paused and looked right at me. She started to walk right at me and turned her head so she was looking right at my face. She knew I was there and that I had nowhere to go.

'You won't win with me boy,' she muttered.

The town started to melt away from me and I knew the power of the blue tea was starting to wear off. I closed my eyes and when I opened them again I was back in Uncle Barry's front room.

'Joe are you ok?' Said Barry.

'I'm fine, just a bit shaken. I'm sure she has just seen me.'

'It's very possible she could have seen you, she has the book and her powers are very strong.'

I need to get as much information from Uncle Barry about this, it's going to get worse as she has the book, we need to stop her.

'Uncle Barry you need to tell me what you know?'

'Yes Joe of course'

Uncle Barry started to tell me that this all started back in the past with what I had seen from drinking the different teas I had tried yesterday and today. The woman I had seen was a witch but a good witch with great manners who would have helped anyone.

This all changed on the day her Mum was taken away from her by the towns folk who accused the mother of using black magic. With this accusation came the death sentence. This had caused the change in the young witch, she had turned so evil that she could and never would love again, her heart had turned as black as her soul.

'But how could she be so evil?' I asked

'Well Joe, are you ready to hear her story?'

Chapter 3

THE RETURN OF THE WITCH

The witch had a name and she was called Lady Malaga. She lived with her Mum, her Mum always liked to help others just like a doctor. If anyone was ill she would use good magic, but it had to be on the quiet. She always looked out for her daughter and tried to show her as much as she could to do with magic, but this had to be kept top secret. She would only use good magic to help others, never harm or make bad things happen.

One day as usual Lady Malaga would walk into the village and see if anyone needed help from her mother, her mother was called Margaret, but people would just call her Maggie. Lady Malaga would just walk up to people and ask if they needed any help or their families, in return they would give them a loaf of bread or a couple of eggs. Sometimes if the families didn't have much themselves, she would only take a few slices of bread. She was just such a kind hearted person and wouldn't want anyone going without. She would just return back home and would tell her Mum if there were any families that were in need of help.

The next day came and the same thing would happen but this day was different as someone was watching everything going on knowing something was not quite right. They reported this to the head of the village. These were the ones who controlled everything that went on in the village and made all the rules. Everyone was far too scared to break the rules and they all knew performing magic came with a death sentence.

News spread around the village like wild fire and it wasn't long before Maggie finally realised that she had to protect her daughter, she knew this would take time and the protection she was planning would take a few days to put into place.

When Maggie practiced good magic they would use a book bound in white and Maggie called this her white book. She knew that eventually nothing good would come of this and recognised her fate. Her daughter would need a lot more than the white book and to offer and that the love for her daughter outweighed the risk of creating more powerful spells that would be needed. Maggie spent all that day and well into the night creating a new book. She was so very pleased with herself but also scared because she knew this was good but could become bad. She would not take any risks when it came to protecting her daughter and she needed this book to be very powerful. She would sacrifice herself to get this book completed. The final step in the creation of the book would be a life force needed to keep the book powerful. Maggie slid a knife across her palm and let the blood flow freely through its paper pages. Maggie knew that her fate had already been sealed and that the towns folk were already on their way. The book had already noticed this and would wait patiently for Maggie to die thus giving the book its full power.

That evening, there was a bang at the door and Maggie knew her time had come. Lady Malaga screamed and lashed out in anger but her Mum told her to stop and that everything would be ok. Some of the towns folk crashed into the cottage and grabbed Maggie and tied up her arms, as Lady Malaga's mother was dragged away she noticed the book on the side but wrapped around it's front cover was a note.

Dear darling, my time has come, I do not want you to worry, the time I'm away I want you to read and learn all of these spells. My darling, this will give you power you wouldn't even begin to think is possible, just be careful where there is great power there will be great danger, you choose your path, I love you, Mum.

This is where the book was created and made by the love of her mother. The deadly magic spells that her Mum put into the book would keep her child safe. She would read the book all day and night and by the time she was ready, she would choose her path. The sweet lovely young lady was no more, she had more power than she could have ever dreamed of. She had people at her feet, she was the queen of evil and no one would cross her. Her Mum had made a sweet daughter become an evil witch. No one dared cross her and the village she lived in become her own town. She also turned the people's minds against them and made them her slaves. If you didn't like anything she would reach into your body and take away your soul and keep it locked away in her sealed room. Where she would keep you there for ever, never seeing your loved ones again. The evil witch was really wicked.

'So Joe there you have it, do you see why we need to keep possession on the book?'

'Yes for sure, how do we find her and the book?'

'She will find you don't worry, we just have to be ready, you cant leave our side Joe.'

"Barry that is enough, you're scaring Joe" Mum says.

'He needed to know.' replied Barry.

I wished the day that the beam of light had appeared, had never happened. I would give anything to be back in my house going about my usual daily routine. I really wanted to see my Dad, he needed to come and see us right now. I needed some fresh air so I headed out into the garden and the sunshine. As I walked outside I could see some little shiny stones floating in the distance and a black cat sat perched on the garden wall staring at me and not moving another cell of its body. All of a sudden it jumped off the wall and walked off.

'Mum Mum.' I shouted back towards the house. Mum came running outside and raced to my side and asked,

'Yes Joe?'

'There was a cat sitting looking at me which then just walked off.'

Mum pulled me with her and dashed inside, shouting at Uncle Barry that it was her. I overheard the conversation between my Mum and Uncle Barry saying that it was not safe outside and that she was watching our every move. My heart was racing once again and I felt on the edge of a panic attack and that my heart could beat right out of my chest.

'Get up stairs Joe' Uncle Barry shouted at me. Mum and I ran up the stairs and then Mum shouted down to my Uncle to get my Dad home as we needed him here now.

Jake was my Dad and I needed to see him, I agreed that we needed Dad home as I felt this would get a lot worse. Time ticked by so slowly and Mum and I were just sitting on my bed, we both slowly began to calm down and it was like we were back in time before this had all happened when we would spend hours just chatting about different things. Not only was my Mum, my Mum but she was also my best friend. Uncle Barry knocked on my bedroom door and said he had spoken to my Dad and that he was on his way back as he knew about the beams of light and knew that she was here. Dad had told Uncle Barry that it could take him around two days to get back and I knew we had no choice but to wait. I couldn't wait to see Dad and ask him all about what was going on. I knew he was trying to track her down but what I didn't understand was why she was back after all these years and who was the man she cursed with eternal life. Where is he and what is his story?

Two days passed and we were all awaiting my Dad's return. The last two days had been very strange, no more talk about anything that had happened or was going to happen. It all went quiet. I took my mind off the things that had happened by playing my computer game. I never saw the cat when I was allowed outside for my daily bit of exercise. Uncle Barry was quiet at meal times and there was no eye contact or any talking. It was like everything that had happened was a dream and that it hadn't happened at all. The only way I knew that this had really happened and that it wasn't a dream was because we were still in Uncle Barry's house. At lunchtime that day, there was a loud crunching of gravel that sounded like someone was driving up towards the house. I ran up to the window to look out onto the drive and saw that it was my Dad pulling up. Mum and I rushed outside to greet my Dad but excitement got the best of my Mum and as she reached my Dad she started screaming out that she was glad he was home and that he was back. Dad wrapped his arms around my Mum and whispered into her ear that it was going to be ok now that he was home. Dad made his way into the kitchen and his eyes searched me out.

'Come here Son, I've missed you so much.'

I walked up to my Dad and wrapped my arms around him and suddenly felt a little safer.

'Dad I'm so glad your home, We need to find her and get the book back that she has taken from us.'

Dad looked at me and smiled

'Don't you worry about it Joe.'

As my Dad said I was not going to worry about anything. Dad was going to keep us all calm and sort everything out. I didn't want to go on at my Dad with everything that Uncle Barry had told me as Dad had only been back with us for such little time.

'Barry' Dad shouted out.

'Yes Jake.'

'Grab me a beer, I think we need to talk.'

This is not fair, Dad has only just come back and now he was going to be speaking with Uncle Barry for such a long time. I guess they do need to come up with a plan. I will leave them to it and go and play my game again. I love playing as it takes my mind off everything. I got lost in playing my game, I checked my watch and saw that two hours had passed, where did all that time go. I jumped out of my skin as my Dad shouted for me to come downstairs.

When i got downstairs, Dad said. 'Right, we have come up with a plan. Please listen to us now son, Barry hasn't told you everything as he wanted me to tell you myself. Grab a chair please Joe, we need to talk.'

There can't be anymore stuff to know, this can't be right but the look on my Dad's face told me everything I needed to know, that this was far from over and that Uncle Barry had only just scratched the surface with what I'm going to learn. Mum shouts at me to see what I was doing and to pick up a chair. I set the chair down beside my Dad in the kitchen. Mum placed a fresh beer beside my Dad, I guess he needs it as he is going through a tough time with everything that is going on.

'Right Joe, I haven't been honest with you with where I have been and what I have been doing. Please believe me when I say this was for your safety but you're going to find out all about this now. Are you ready?'

'I guess so Dad.' I replied.

Chapter 4

DADS HOME

'When I was your age, I found myself in the same situation as you find yourself in now Joe, this witch has been around for a very long time and time after time she keeps finding her way back. At first she was not that powerful but as time has gone on she has gained her full strength and her powers are beyond belief. We have been looking for her for years but we have never found any leads or pointers to see where she was hiding until now. Something happened when that beam of light filled the sky, the light was her book bringing her back with even more power than even she has ever experienced herself. We are not entirely sure how this has happened but we have been planning this for many years. Whispers have echoed around the world saying that as soon as you turned of age she would return and that she needs something from you. We are not sure what this is and we don't really want to find out. Your Mum and I will keep you safe. Please don't panic Joe, we will never let anything happen to you.'

As you can imagine I didn't know what to think, but as my Dad had said I was in safe hands and I had to go along with everything I was told. Dad gave me a set of instructions that I had to abide to to protect my safety. I was to stay in the house at all times and not go outside unless I had one of the adults with me because this witch could be anywhere.

'Wont I see her though?' I asked my Dad.

'Joe what you have to understand is what you might see isn't always the case and could be an illusion, she is very strong and to get what she wants, she will do any thing.'

'You mean like when I saw the cat, and that was her?'

'Yes my point, exactly Joe.'

I turn to look at my Mum in the background and she is waving her arms around and shaking her head to Uncle Barry. I finally understand this is not like an adventure from my video games this is real and it's really happening. I wanted to know what the witch wanted with me and what would she do to me if she ever got to me. Dad got up and walked to the fridge to grab another beer. He offered one to Uncle Barry who said 'no thanks.'

Mum came over towards me I noticed the worried expression that marked her face, she pulled up a chair and said 'I can't believe she is back after all this time, what the hell does she want?' I begin to think should I sit here and listen to more or head up to bed and try and take my mind off the things that are happening all around me. There was a loud bang as Uncle Barry fell to the floor, each of us jumped a mile as we were not expecting anything to happen. Dad turned to see what had caused Uncle Barry to fall but he was on the floor wriggling around laughing his head off, gasping for breath trying to keep up with the laughter. This was all so very odd and strange and Uncle Barry was not one of those people you would expect this behaviour from.

Uncle Barry sat up, even though he was still laughing, All of a sudden the laughter stopped and the look upon Uncle Barry's face told us that he thought it was strange we were not laughing with him. He was so strange how he just hit the floor. Uncle Barry turned his head around that fast, I thought he would have injured himself and spoke directly at my Dad.

'You won't win I will take your boy and I have my book.'

As soon as this happened Uncle Barry stood back up and started to shake his head side to side like he was trying to get rid of something that had taken over him. He was unaware of what had just happened. He told us that he had a bad headache and was going to lie down. This was all beginning to get out of hand, how was this witch using Uncle Barry's body to get to all of us.

Dad turns to my Mum and says 'It's time to get planning now, we have done it before and we have to be strong again. We will beat her for good this time.'

I could tell my Mum was in no mood to respond to anyone at this point. She wanted to make sure that we were all going to be ok, so she just shook her head at my Dad and said nothing. I don't think my Mum had come to terms with the eventuality that this witch was back haunting our family. Dad repeated that we can do this again like we have done before. I really wanted to find out more but I know now was not the time and we had all had enough for one day. Mum offered everyone some hot chocolate to take up to bed. I loved my Mum's hot chocolate and this would make it all the more easier to fall asleep after the drama that the day brought with it. There was so much going through my head but my body was telling me exhaustion was creeping up on me. I didn't know what each day would bring from now onwards but all I was hoping for would be for this witch to be defeated once and for all.

As I lay in bed that night, all I could think was why she was after me, what had I ever done to her and was she really that bad. I had a feeling I needed to have some more of Uncle Barry's tea and step back into the past to try and see if I had missed anything that could help me in the future. It was a little after midnight and I knew my brain would not let my body relax enough to enter the realm of sleep. I heard a noise outside my bedroom window and I quickly turned over to try and trick my brain into thinking I had not heard anything but the noise was getting louder and louder. I could make out that is was someone calling my name and I knew who the voice belonged to. I got out of bed and looked out of my bedroom window, it was that dark all I could make out was the features of a lady. Was this the witch or was this some illusion playing tricks with me. I had a good look out of the window but could not make out who it was. I opened the window and leaned out to see if I could see anything more and the voice said 'It's ok Joe, it's only Mum, come on down.'

I could suddenly hear my Dad's words of warning from earlier on about not going outside unless I was with one of them. This was my Mum so it should be ok to go and get her. I slid on my dressing gown and toed into some slippers that were at the end of the bed. I yanked open my bedroom door and went to meet my Mum. I crept down the hallway as I didn't want to wake anyone else. I could hear Dad and Uncle Barry snoring away. I then asked myself, why was my Mum outside and what was she doing? I slowly walked down the stairs and remembered to step down the one step that would make a loud creaking sound. I reached the bottom of the stairs and then a loud voice sounded from behind me.

'What are you doing out of bed and where do you think you are going?'

I turned and looked up the stairs and there stood my Mum and she did not look at all happy. I had to do a double take as I knew my Mum was outside asking me to go outside with her. I didn't say this to my Mum at all as I did not want to burden her with more stress, so i made something up quickly. 'I was going to make a drink in the kitchen,' I replied to my Mum.

My Mum raised one of her eyebrows and said 'Ok then straight to bed Joe, it's late.'

This can't be happening to me, I just heard my Mum outside of my bedroom window calling me to go and join her and then all of a sudden she was at the top of the stairs asking what I was doing out of bed. I should have told myself this was a trick and not what was really happening. My mouth had gone so dry I knew I needed some water. I raced to the kitchen and switched on the light but made sure I did not look outside. I grabbed a glass and filled it with water and ran back upstairs into the safety of my bedroom. I needed to start being more careful, like Dad said earlier make sure what I see was real and not just some trick being played on me.

I woke up the next morning and felt totally drained and that I would not be able to get out of bed. The smell of breakfast wafted in through the crack under my bedroom door and my stomach rumbled. I could almost taste the food that I knew my Mum was cooking. I heard her shout up the stairs that breakfast was ready. I quickly got myself dressed and brushed my teeth. I walked down into the kitchen and could see that Dad was already sitting at the table and Mum was cooking at the stove but Uncle Barry was nowhere to be seen, I guessed he was still in bed after the events of yesterday and must be sleeping it all off. Breakfast this morning was eggs on toast with a side of baked beans. Mum passed me a plate which was piled high. I tucked in greedily and turned to look at the newspaper my Dad was reading. The front cover was filled with the story about the beam of light that had filled the sky. The print was so small I could not read what the story was saying. Dad was the first to finish his breakfast and said 'Right, today we are all going to plan what we need to do, is everyone ok with this?'

I shook my head as I was still eating and Mum also shook her head. My Mum seemed a lot better today a lot more head strong. I think the shock of everything that had happened had now settled and my Mum was ready to fight.

'Where is Uncle Barry?' I said.

'He is outside in the outer buildings.' Mum replied.

I was beginning to wonder what Uncle Barry was doing out there and remembered what it was like the first time I had seen the outer building. Dad dropped his newspaper on the table and demanded we all eat up, we had a lot to get on with today.

Dad leapt up from the kitchen table and made his way outside to the outer building I presumed. Mum was busy cleaning up after everyone and loading all the dishes into the dishwasher. I offered Mum some help but she refused. I began slowly making my way outside to find my Dad and Uncle Barry and noticed that my hands were shaking with nerves as I didn't know what was going to happen next. As I crossed over the garden, you would never believe it, but the cat was sitting upon the wall watching my every move again. I ran into the outer building as I thought this must be her. As I entered the outer building, I began to notice the whole room had changed. I could not believe what I was seeing, there were big cages hanging down from the ceiling and lots of different equipment hung on the walls, all of which I had never seen before.

'That is everything Jake' Uncle Barry said.

'Brilliant so are we ready to catch the witch.' replied my Dad.

I could feel myself get oddly excited, here I was just a normal kid so i thought, about to undertake the adventure of a life time. This is the sort of thing that would happen in action movies. I still wanted to find out who the man was that was cursed back in the past and what had happened to him. I needed to speak with Uncle Barry and get some more of his magic tea but how was I going to do this?

'What are you doing boy? Don't just daydream all day, help us will you.'

Why did he always call me boy and help with what, they haven't told me to do anything.

'Yes of course, what do you want me to do?'

'Can you see that pile of wood in the corner there, start by taking it outside please, I want us to have a bonfire tonight, where we can all sit round and come up with some ideas.'

I loved the idea of a bonfire, there was something about an open fire and using long sticks to toast marshmallows. I was suddenly wishing the day away and hoping the sun would set earlier than usual.

'Fire, is that such a good idea?' Dad replies.

'Yes it will be fine. We have all the traps here if anything were to happen, don't panic." Barry said.

'Ok I hope you know what you're doing, you know what happened last time, don't you Barry?'

I'm not too sure what was happening now between my Dad and Uncle Barry. I loved the idea of having a bonfire but after Dad had made those comments I wasn't too sure what was going to happen. It was almost like Uncle Barry was setting a trap for this witch.

'Let's not make a fuss now shall we, take the wood outside boy.' Barry shouts out

I started piling up the wood in my arms and took some of it outside. As I threw the wood down on the floor, I noticed movement in the kitchen window and saw my Mum put her head in her hands. She already knew what was happening this evening and I guessed she didn't think this was a good idea either. I thought all of a sudden that the witch must despise fire because of what happened to her Mum all that time ago. I was starting to worry a little as I made my way back inside the outer building to get some more wood.

'Is this a good idea tonight, with the fire?' I asked Uncle Barry.

The look he gave back to me told me all I needed to know. I began carrying more wood outside to make a pile ready for the bonfire. On top of the wood I had already placed was the black cat from earlier. Again this was sitting so straight and upright and suddenly it began to speak to me. My mouth dropped open in shock, how could a cat be speaking. It warned me that this was a bad idea and that I shouldn't be doing this. After the words of warning it had given, the cat just ran away from me. This time the cat seemed different than before, I began to question myself if this was the same cat as the one perched on the wall earlier. I went back into the outer building to fetch the last bit of wood and could hear my Dad and Uncle Barry having a heated conversation. I knew this was my time to head back into the house.

I walked into the house and there was no sign of Mum. I couldn't get it out of my head that I needed to see more about the past, I wanted and needed to know more. I took it upon myself to go into the kitchen and hunt for the tea that Uncle Barry made me before I didn't have a clue how to make it or what colour I needed it to be. Surely there must be a recipe book of some sort to show me. I looked through every cupboard in the kitchen and the tea was nowhere to be found. I looked upwards and above the stove there was a secret cupboard hidden between two more. I opened up this cupboard and found the tea I was looking for and miraculously sitting beside the tea was a book. I grabbed the book and some tea and ran upstairs to my room. I didn't want to bother anyone else as they all seemed too busy. My stomach was a pit of nerves by the time I had reached my bedroom. Quickly and without changing my mind, I put all of the tea making equipment onto my bed. Amongst all the different bits and pieces it was a purple jar that caught my eye. I opened the book and began to read how to prepare the tea. The book was full of instructions and do's and don'ts. I began to read, past life is not a game and you should proceed carefully and err on the side of caution. The blue and red tea will show you so much but the purple tea is the most powerful option. A word of warning for those who use the purple tea, you can and will be seen, the red and blue tea keeps you safely hidden.

There is a lot more of the book but I knew straight away that I wanted to use the purple tea no matter what, I wanted and needed to find out more. I quickly ran downstairs to boil some water. The kettle seemed like it was taking ages to boil but I was finally on my way back upstairs to my bedroom with some boiling water. As I got back into my bedroom, I heard the door slam shut downstairs. Uncle Barry and Dad must have come back inside, a small part of me was thinking, when I drink the purple tea what if I am gone for a very long time in the past, what if I can't get back. I had hastily made the decision to grab this tea and equipment from the kitchen and believed I was very foolish in jeopardising my safety. How was I going to get all of this stuff back into the kitchen without anyone knowing I had taken it.

'Joe where are you?' Someone shouted.

I wasn't sure who it was, and in a blind moment of panic I grabbed everything and hid it under my bed. I went onto the landing to see who was calling me and nobody was there. This was oddly strange as someone had just shouted me and I had heard the door slam but all of the rooms were empty. I couldn't work out what was going on. I searched the whole house for the voice that had shouted me but I could not find anyone. I finally made my way into the kitchen and looked around as this was not Uncle Barry's kitchen. Where was I and what was happening. Suddenly everything started to change and swirl around me. I was so confused with everything that was happening. Little did I know how powerful the purple tea actually was, that's why it was sealed into a tiny little jar. It has it's own mind, but I was foolish and had touched the bottle when I had taken it out of the cupboard. Was this the past again or was this something new I was about to discover?

Chapter 5

TEA OF MAGIC

The rules of the magic are inside the book, the red and blue tea will show you the past but keep you concealed from everyone. This magic would only last up to an hour. The purple tea was a lot more powerful and it could take you anywhere you would like to go, this tea has it's own life force and power. The book read that this jar must not be opened if you didn't know it's true power and that this magic could get you stuck in the past for 48 hours. I didn't realise that in the blind moment of panic that the jar had come open a little and the magic of the purple tea had started to work without me knowing. Where had I been taken?

I walked towards the window and could see it looked like the village I had visited previously, I walked to the front door and this house lead out onto the village square where the witch's mother was sentenced to death, this was also the place she has caged that man for eternity. I knew I had to be careful not to be seen, just seeing this place again had given me the creeps. You could still feel how much rage she had and how truly evil she had become. I can remember that this was the time she was about to cast her spell on the man. I needed to get up close with the man so I could ask him some things and with the power of the purple tea, this would be possible as he would be able to see and speak back to me. This was going to be my only chance, the witch had turned to leave so I crept slowly towards the cage that was holding the man prisoner. He was trying his best to escape and the cage was getting more powerful by the minute, the more the man struggled, the brighter green the cage around him become. Now was my only chance as the witch had disappeared, I made a dash towards the cage and suddenly the man turned and spotted me.

'What are you doing?gGet away from here now.' he shouts.

I wouldn't be able to let this go, I needed to find out.

'Don't worry she has gone and I need to help you get out of this and ask you some questions.'

At this point the man didn't look too impressed, he had just been caged by an evil witch and now a strange boy wanted to ask questions.

'Ok, you can help me, over there is my briefcase, go inside and you should see a clear box."

I went inside and grabbed the clear box.

'Yes I have it.'

'Good, now place the box beside the green cage for me.'

I placed the clear box by the cage and suddenly the box sprung to life and stated to suck the cage inside the box. Once the cage had disappeared the box closed its lid and snapped a lock to keep the green swirling magic inside.

'Wow that was so good.'

'Thank you boy, I would have done it myself you know, I didn't need your help.'

I started to laugh at how the man thought he would have been able to help himself. His briefcase was out of his reach. Suddenly a thought popped into my head, if I hadn't of helped this man now, who did help out in the past?

'We have to stop her.' He shouted.

'Excuse me sir, do you mind me asking what is your name?'

"Of course young man, my name is Barry."

My mouth just dropped open, was this Uncle Barry? Now this is where this gets even stranger. I couldn't ask anymore questions at this point as we needed to hunt down this witch and stop her once and for all. We started walking up through the village and people were dashing around in a blind panic, they were scared that the witch wanted revenge. The man known as Barry was looking for signs of her everywhere muttering a strange language as he went. The trees that once stood green and proud were now falling to the ground and the trickling of the town square fountain had fallen silent and no water flowed. The water had turned a brown murky colour and moss had started to stagnant over the surface. People lay motionless all through the village, had death claimed them when the witch had started to exact her revenge! Barry told me that they were still alive but just in a sleeping state, this was a spell that the witch had cast before you disappeared. We need to find and stop her. I carried on following Barry to the end of the village and bending off to the left looked like there was a path leading into the woods, this is where she must have gone.

As Barry was leading the way down the path he said. 'She must be down this way, I have to stop her.'

As I went to reply a funny feeling started sweeping from the tips of my fingers down to my toes. I looked up and had realised the man I was following had vanished and the woods had started to fall away and the picture had again started to change. How was this possible, the purple tea was meant to be stronger and last longer, I was not ready to leave yet. I needed to find the witch and stop this once and for all. I start to look around and my room comes back into view and I lay on my bed with Mum, Dad and Uncle Barry all standing around me.

'What have you done Joe?' Mum shouts out.

'It's ok both of you go, down stairs i'll sort this out.' Barrys says.

Mum and Dad both left the room and went downstairs. I looked up at Uncle Barry and I didn't know what to say. He was going to be so angry with me for taking the purple tea without asking. What was I going to do, he looked so angry?

'Joe I understand what you have done and I knew you would do this, I was waiting for this to happen and waiting for you. I now understand that you know who I am, you helped me escape years ago Joe. You are very special and even before you were born you were always around.'

I don't understand but I know I have a big part to play here.

'Joe, I need you to keep this to yourself please, I don't want to freak anyone out.'

'Yes Uncle Barry I understand, but you need to let me tell you what I saw.'

'Joe my boy, I already know.'

'Well I didn't see what happened and if you caught the witch?'

'Joe I did indeed this is what happened.'

I followed the path that went into the woods. There I saw a cottage, surrounding the cottage were lots of trees that were just broken old pieces of wood, no leaves on them whatsoever. They had been positioned to look like this was a protection spell she had conjured, and turned the trees into weapons. As I was walking towards the cottage, I stood on something that made a noise, within seconds the cottage door flew open. The witch knew someone was there, with a wave of her hand she brought the trees to life, they sprung up and guarded her and wielded their branches like they were knives. I knew I was in a dangerous situation and I had no other choice than to retreat back into the safety of the village.

I headed back into the village to get some help from other people, by this time it was too late, she was on her way into the village with an army of the killing trees, right before my eyes people were being hunted down like dogs, we couldn't stop her, this was the end of our village and people. I was helping so many people get back into the safety of their homes, trying to protect them. Suddenly the trees dropped to the ground like a fly losing the will to live. The witch had so much pent up rage she had burnt the trees with a spell. Suddenly with a flash of light a figure appeared, it was the witch's mother. She cast a spell of her daughter which transported and trapped her in a far away land. The mother knew she had taken this a step too far but her spell would keep the witch away from others for many years to come. She turned to me with what time she had left and made me promise to protect and guard the book with my life. She explained that every one hundred years her spell would waiver and that her daughter the witch would return. We come to know the witch as Lady Malaga and this is the witch you have been seeing lately.

'Where do I come into this then Uncle Barry.' I said.

'Your soul Joe, is from a very long time ago, you also live on, each time you come back you can't remember anything but as time goes on you do too.'

This cannot be true, if I lived on just like Uncle Barry had just told me, I would remember snippets of my old lives but I can't remember anything. I have had the odd sense of Deja Vu but everyone experiences this in their life time. I try to remember but all I can remember are memories of the lifetime and nothing from anytime before.

'Uncle Barry if I live on just like her, what does the witch want from me?'

'Joe, there is something I want you to see, but this might scare you a little, this will show you who you were in your past.'

Uncle Barry reaches into his pocket and pulls out a yellow tea bag, from the long coat he was wearing.

'I want you to drink this tea tonight Joe, make it just before you go to bed. I must warn you that you can't change anything at all when you go back as this could have many damaging affects for the future. Are you listening Joe?'

'Yes I won't do anything that would jeopardise our future.'

'You must look into your past as this will aid your future, but don't change anything.'

'Ok Uncle Barry.'

'Good lad.'

Uncle Barry walks out of the room and heads downstairs, I'm sat here holding the tea bag in shock and thinking about the adventure tonight will bring. As night time starts to set over Uncle Barry's house, I head up to my room with a cup of boiled water ready for my adventure with the yellow tea bag. I have a funny feeling this will change everything but I need to find out what I was back in the past and why does Lady Malaga want me so much. I let the tea bag soak for a minute as I get ready for bed, suddenly there is a loud smash as my cup along with the tea crashes to the floor. I looked in horror and could have cried out. There was a cat in my room standing on the dresser where my tea was just moments before, the cat did this but why? I ran over to the smashed cup and as I did the cat jumped out of the window. I think this was a warning from the cat that I shouldn't have seen something in my past. I go downstairs to grab some cleaning stuff and see Uncle Barry was sitting on the sofa.

'Well boy what are you doing up, you should be looking into your past, like I told you to.'

'I was going too, then the cat smashed the cup off of the side.'

'Done what boy, that was the last of my yellow tea.'

'It wasn't my fault.'

'Well I can make some more of it, but it will take me a few days to make. No worries boy, don't forget the fire soon'

I completely forgot about the fire tonight, I really hope nothing happens, I needed to get changed into something a bit warmer, as the wind was picking up outside. The weather didn't look good at all as I was getting changed and I had a feeling that something wasn't right. Why does Uncle Barry want me to go back in the past so much? Is there something he wants me to remember?

As I was walking down the stairs, I could smell the burning wood from the fire. I looked through the window and the flames were flickering so high that at one point I thought that it would burst through the window. I could see Mum, Dad and Uncle Barry outside, something inside me was telling me that we needed to stop this as something bad was going to happen. Mum had cooked us all burgers for dinner but all I wanted to do was to stay inside as the feeling in my stomach was telling me that the fire was a totally bad idea. This felt like a trap had been set to catch Lady Malaga. Mum was happy that she had cooked us all a lovely meal and Dad and Uncle Barry were drinking beer as usual whilst sitting around the fire. In the corner of my eye I saw a flash of something in the flames of the fire, I ran outside shouting for everyone to get away from the fire, I knew something was going to happen and I was right. For some reason everyone wasn't listening to me and they just stared into the fire, it was almost like they were drawn to it like moths to flames. No one could stop them as they inched ever closer to the fire. Mum was holding a plate and suddenly this dropped to the floor with an almighty crash, the sound brought Mum to her senses and she started to shout at Dad and Barry to get away from the fire but even this would not wake them from the spell that I guessed was happening.

The flames started to get higher by the second and this was starting to scare me, the flames seemed to be blowing towards Dad and Uncle Barry. Both of them were still walking towards the fire and everything that was going on seemed unreal and that it shouldn't be happening. In the middle of the flames an outline of a person had started to appear and I knew this was the dreaded Lady Malaga. Suddenly the centre of the fire disappeared and there in her black dress stood Lady Malaga, the crackling of the fire died away and all you could hear was the evil laugh coming from within her. She turned her head towards me and said. 'You stupid boy, no one can save you, not even your parents. You're mine!"

Seconds later the flames died down completely and Lady Malaga had vanished from the flames. Our bonfire was back to being a normal little fire and Dad and Uncle Barry were totally unaware of what had happened. Mum looked at me and said that dinner was ready. I looked down to the floor where the plate Mum was holding just smashed and there was nothing there. Was this all a dream and had what I saw really happened or was my imagination running wild again. I started to believe that Lady Malaga was haunting me or playing tricks on my mind. I know for a fact I saw my Mum drop the plate and saw it smash into little pieces, I was not getting what was happening around me.

'Joe come and help take the dinner out and don't forget the camp chairs.'

'Yes Mum, Oh Mum! Where are the camp chairs?'

'Under the stairs Joe, now hurry up before the food gets cold.'

I reply yes to my Mum but she must know I have never been here before and I am learning where things are every day. As I walk towards the stairs, there is that cat again sitting outside the cupboard, I need to know who or what this cat is. As I get nearer to the chat, it starts grinning at me and says 'I warned you about your fire earlier on didn't I?'

After this the cat does it's usual running off trick but I thought to myself not this time.

'Wait don't go, I want to speak to you.' I shouted after the cat.

The cat stopped abruptly and turned it's head and replied 'You want to talk to me? No one ever wants to talk to me, they are usually more scared of me. What do you want to ask me?'

'Who are you and why do you come and talk to me?'

'Do you really need to ask that? I'm looking out for you, all will be made clear, I've got to go she's watching me!'

'Just wait a minute will you.' I shout after the cat

'All will make sense when you drink the yellow tea.' The cat muttered as it walked away.

The yellow tea is the key to what seems like everything, I really hope Uncle Barry will be able to make some more but wait a minute, the cat told me to drink the yellow tea. That was the same one the cat had smashed earlier on, was Lady Malaga playing even more tricks on my mind or was she turning herself into a cat to trick me into thinking I could trust it. I heard my Mum shout for the camping chairs, as I had momentarily forgotten about them. I shouted towards the garden that I am coming. As I walked out into the garden all I could smell was my favourite meal that Mum would cook on occasions. Hamburgers were the meal I loved so much. I look over at Uncle Barry and he smirks at me, I am starting to think that Uncle Barry is warming up to me as I am him. We all sit around the fire laughing, joking and eating the most amazing food. My mind starts to wander and I begin to think about the argument that Dad and Uncle Barry had had earlier on. We had been sitting outside for most of the evening and the weather had been on our side but Mum wanted to go inside and relax, so both her and my Dad head back into the house. As they both leave Uncle Barry says for me to follow him into the outer building.

'Now listen boy, I will be out here for a few days now, I need to make you some more yellow tea, I do not want to be disturbed, I will come to you when it's done.'

'No problem Uncle Barry, do you want me to keep Mum and Dad away as well?'

'Yes that's what I was going to say, keep them away too, make things up if you have to, this is our secret.'

I thought this as well, so I knew I would try my best for my Uncle Barry. I told him that I would do anything I could to keep Mum and Dad from disturbing him. I left Uncle Barry and started to walk back towards the house. My Uncle's sense of humour did make me laugh, you would never know where you stood with him. You also didn't know if he was happy or not but he was good to us. I began to wonder if Dad knew that he was the one who the witch cursed all those years ago and how did Uncle Barry know how to use magic. I started to go towards my room and started to plan some ideas how to help out Uncle Barry.

Chapter 6

IDEAS

The next morning had come and something odd was happening. There was no smell of breakfast which I would usually smell and I hadn't heard Mum call me down for breakfast. As I lay in bed I wasn't thinking much of it as I had to come up with ideas to stop Mum and Dad finding out what Uncle Barry was doing. I spent a few minutes coming up with some ideas but I needed to find out what was happening downstairs, this was not normal because I would usually have heard or smelt what was going on downstairs.

I got up and put my dressing gown on and opened my bedroom door, the silence in the house was very creepy. I made my way downstairs and there was no one around, where was every one? I could hear Uncle Barry outside and started to wonder if I should go out and tell Uncle Barry but I remembered him telling me last night that he did not want to be disturbed under any circumstance. I was at a loss on what to do. I suddenly had a thought to go out onto the drive to see if there were any cars, that would tell me if Mum and Dad were still here. I wretched open the front door and made my way outside. There were no cars on the drive, why would

Mum and Dad have left so early it was still very early. They must have had somewhere important to be so I made my way inside the house and started to make my own breakfast. I made a cup of tea and just toast. As I sat at the table eating breakfast, I started going over my plans to guard Uncle Barry. So far so easy with Mum and Dad being out of the way, but I have to remain on look out. Hopefully Uncle Barry can finish the tea in a few days otherwise Mum and Dad will become suspicious with what's going on.

Also the weeks holiday from school is nearly up, what will I do about going to school, as I can't be out of my Mum and Dad's sight as it's not safe, as the witch might come after me. I really need to start calling her by her name Lady Malaga. The name just sends shivers down my spine. Suddenly I realised that I had put too much butter on my toast as it was dripping everywhere. I had to be careful not to get it anywhere on Uncle's Barry's furniture as he would not be pleased at all. I decided to go and get a shower and get ready then by the time I would be ready Mum and Dad would surely be back. After a few hours chilling out in my room, I started to worry about where my parents were. Suddenly I hear a noise from downstairs, could this be them. I shouted down to see if this was them but I got no response. This was very strange as the house seemed so quiet. I was sure this was them as I heard noises from downstairs. I made my way downstairs and into the kitchen. Across the kitchen floor was a creepy shadow and I knew instantly this was too tall to be either of my parents. It could have been Uncle Barry as he was slightly taller than both my parents, bet it's Uncle Barry.

'Uncle Barry, is that you?'

No answer from him either. Come on Joe you've got this, just walk into the kitchen, there is nothing to be scared of. I walked into the kitchen and saw this was not Uncle Barry either. The figure span around so quickly because I must have startled him.

'Who are you?' he asked dressed in a brown long coat, with a tall hat.

'I'm Joe sir, what are you doing in my Uncle's house?'

'I did knock but there was no answer, I came in to see Barry, I'm his good friend Bill.'

'Nice to meet you Bill, Uncle Barry is out in the outer building.'

At this point I didn't know if to let Bill go and see Uncle Barry or if I should make something up quickly. I decided to go with my distraction plans as Uncle Barry did say that he did not want to be disturbed by anyone at all. I needed to make something up quickly so I offered Bill a cup of tea and that I would get Uncle Barry for him. Bill agreed and made himself comfortable in the living room and shouted back into the kitchen that he takes his tea strong with two sugars. This plan was going well and Bill was listening to me, what I will say to him is that I went out to speak with my Uncle and that he was too busy and that he will call Bill later on today.

As I was making the tea, I saw Uncle Barry coming out of the outer buildings, I didn't see what he was doing but there was some kind of smoke, it was yellow in colour and becoming quickly out of control. I am guessing that Uncle Barry had nearly completed the magic, the smoke was bellowing out from the outer buildings and started to cover the garden. At one point it almost came through the kitchen window, I reached to shut the window quick, before Bill saw and became suspicious of my plan to keep my Uncle on his task at hand. It then hit me what if Uncle Barry had made something up to Mum and Dad so they wouldn't be aware what was going on today?

Uncle Barry looked up and saw me through the kitchen window, he put his thumb up to me with a smile on his face, I got the impression that everything was going well and starting to work, the yellow tea would be ready soon. After the kettle had boiled I made the tea for Bill and went in search of him in the living room. He wasn't in there and nowhere to be seen. This was odd as I had heard him call back from the living room so I didn't understand where he had gone, did he see the yellow smoke and start to investigate it for himself. The front door banged open and Uncle Barry walked in.

'The plan is going really well, I sent your parents off on an errand earlier on this morning, as we don't want them to know what we are up to now do we? Making yellow tea is always a messy business and with all that smoke I wouldn't have kept it much of a secret would I? I needed to keep it hidden.'

'Thats great Uncle Barry, I was getting worried where Mum and Dad were, but this makes total sense now. Who's Bill, Uncle?'

'I don't know a Bill, what are you going on about Joe.'

'Your good friend Bill came and visited you earlier, I offered him some tea as I didn't want to disturb you.'

At this point I knew something was going on, I explained to my Uncle what had gone on this morning, with Bill popping in and asking for some tea and going to sit in the living room. I looked at my Uncle's face and could see complete rage fall over his facial expressions. He was not happy at all and made a dash to the nearest window to look back towards the outer building and shouted out in anger when he saw what was going on outside. Uncle Barry began to walk back outside and turned to shout at me, he said that I should have got him straight away and that his work was being destroyed.

I raced to the kitchen myself and the yellow smoke from earlier on had all but disappeared and in its place was a big cloud of black smoke, snaking its way around the outer building, as it touched the outer buildings, they disintegrated and turned into a dirty black dust.

I couldn't believe what was happening, I didn't know that Bill wasn't in fact a friend of my Uncle's, she's tricked me again. Was I always going to be on the back foot when it came to her? Lady Malaga had been here again and she was a lot more powerful then I originally thought. She must have been watching what was going on and felt threatened by the making of the yellow tea. She obviously could change into anything she wanted to at will, to be able to corrupt minds and trick people to wreak havoc where she could. I ran after my Uncle and told him that I was sorry but I didn't want to disturb him when he was working. Uncle Barry got to the outer building to try and save his work from utter disaster but it was too late. The spell she had cast over the building was too strong and all that was left was an empty shell held up by the original foundations of the building.

Suddenly a cruel high pitched evil laugh filled the air and I instantly knew she was still here looking at the chaos she had caused. She issued a warning to both me and my uncle.

'You thought you could defeat me did you, stupid silly fools.' Her laughter echoed all around us.

The cloud of black smoke was crawling and creeping across the garden, the once lush green grass turned a filthy dark brown as soon as the smoke touched it. Uncle Barry shouted out to get out of the way as the black smoke started to inch towards the house. The smoke licked up the side of the house and I watched in utter amazement as the bricks started to crumble. The laughter was getting louder by the minute and I could hear a faint echo of the word fools. I ran into the house closely followed by Uncle Barry. The smoke made its way into the kitchen, ripping up the floorboards in its wake, the smoke was filing the room, just making its way across the floor causing utter destruction. I didn't know what to do other than watch in amazement at this pure show of power. Suddenly the house started to shake, the sofa being pushed from side to side like it weighed nothing. Pictures on the wall swaying from side to side until eventually the slid off the nails that help them in place. Was this the end and was I ever going to see my parents again? As quick as the house started to shake, it stopped and the cruel echo of the voice filled the house and told us that we had been warned.

As the smoke started to disappear, I could make out Lady Malaga in the distance standing outside. Uncle Barry run towards her but with a flick of her wrist she surrounded herself in a dark bubble, whilst laughing at the feeble attempt of my uncle. There was now no way my Uncle could get to her and stop her. The more he tried the more she laughed and flicked my Uncle away from her. Time and time again for her amusement. She spoke out but this time her voice was different, everything she was saying made its way through the walls and felt like the house was full of her warnings. I heard her say in the background that she would win this time.

I could see my Uncle Barry getting weaker by the minute as he tried to stop her, but this was not going to end anytime soon. I watched as she made her way towards me and anything in her path was pushed out of the way like it barely weighed anything. Some things were crushed with the sudden impact and full force of her magic. I could feel her power as I tried to make my escape, suddenly I felt like something was pulling me back towards her, I could feel her breath on the back of my neck. I felt her hand grab around my wrist and whispered into my ear 'You want to know the truth do you? Let me show you.'

I felt the floor fall away from my feet, and I was falling into a dark abyss, the voice in my head started to laugh again and say come with me. In the background I could hear my Uncle Barry shout for me to not look at anything and for me to close my eyes. Suddenly the dark face went to a place filled with light, there was blue sky and green trees as far as the eye could see. It was so incredibly beautiful that I almost forgot that I had been captured by Lady Malaga. I suddenly remembered my Uncle's warning to keep my eyes shut, so I shut them instantly. Her voice filled my ears demanding that I opened my eyes but I just ignored it and kept my eyes shut as tight as I could. I could feel her breath on my face and her voice shouted even louder for me to get my eyes open. I ignored her requests and all of a sudden the falling stopped and I heard her scream out.

This made me open my eyes and I was back in my Uncle's garden and my Uncle stood looking all around. I looked to see if Lady Malaga was there and she was nowhere to be seen.

'Good lad you kept your eyes shut, she nearly had you in her own world, where she could keep you there. The spell only works if you keep your eyes open, it is where she keeps her prisoners, but it didn't work on you, you are more powerful than you think Joe.'

'I almost kept my eyes open Uncle, there was something inside me saying to keep them open.'

'Yes that's what the spell does, it makes you see things. Once you open your eyes she will trap you in her world. It's a very strong spell, but you Joe are different, this is why I want you to go back into the past and remember what you used to do.'

'What do you mean, what I used to do?'

'Joe you were very powerful in your past, you used to create your own spells. With each life you live you forget more and more of your old life. This is why she wants to catch you, as you could be the only one to defeat her and she knows this.'

'Cool Barry, was I able to do magic before?'

'Yes you did, she will be back for you, you have to be ready Joe. I need to make this yellow tea, but she will know, Joe you need to remember how to do a spell to hide what we do. You know deep down what it is, I need you to think if you have had any strange dreams, as this could be a clue to the spell, without you knowing'

'I will try Barry, what are we going to do with all the mess and the writing on all the walls?"

'There's nothing we can do Joe, the spell is so powerful you can't get rid of them, but I know who can.'

'Joe my boy there's so much you haven't been told, your Mum and Dad are not just any one, they also know the secrets of magic. This has been kept from you until the time is right, they knew all about what I was doing, this was a test to see if you can withhold the secrets of magic.'

'What do you mean a test?'

'To see if you were ready, they knew that if I made the yellow tea, this will bring Lady Malaga to us. We knew there were risks with this, as we knew she wanted to trap you in her world. I knew you would be ready for this Joe, your Mum and Dad were panicking about this day, but I knew deep down you were ready.'

I could have dropped to the floor in amazement at this point, Uncle Barry was using me like a guinea pig but I could understand and see the reasons why.

'Thanks for that Uncle Barry, so that was the real Lady Malaga then?'

I had to ask him this as I didn't think he could have created all that had happened with his magic all for the sakes of a test or could he?

'That Joe, I will leave up to you, I do know a lot of spells so I will let you decide.'

I wasn't best pleased at this point.

'So where are Mum and Dad then?'

'They have been here the whole time Joe, watching and assessing you through your test.'

So all that had happened was not real and all created with the illusion of magic. I looked around and could still see the floor boards ripped up and the writing all over the walls. Pictures lay at the foot of the walls where they had been flung from the walls. How was this all staged, this I will never know. Lady Malaga likes to confuse and trick your mind and by the looks of things so does Uncle Barry. I was adamant this was real as I felt her breath on my neck and her hands around my arm. The laughter filled the air and so did the black smoke. The more days I spent at Uncle Barry's house things were just getting weirder and weirder. I have never liked school back in my old life but I would give anything to be back there now and have a normal life.

'Great work son.' Mum shouted out.

'Mum where did you come from? Where is Dad?'

'He's right here next to me.'

'I cant see him.'

'Look harder, he's right here.'

I focused really hard and really looked out for my Dad, so much so that my eyes started to hurt. Suddenly I started to see an outline and then I heard my Dad's voice saying 'Yes son, that's good, I'm right here you can do this.' Was this another test and if it was I had had enough of them by now, this morning had taken its toll on me.

'I can see the outline of you Dad,' as I could see Dad waving back at me.

'That's right, the more you see of me, the more it will show you. Come on son you've got this.'

At this point in this next test, my head exploded in pain as I was straining to see my Dad. Suddenly he came into focus and I could hear the praise in his voice as he said, 'You have done it son.'

My Dad was there along with my Mum and they could make themselves invisible. This was so strangely cool, I would love to learn and know how to use this spell as I could use this at school and be the worlds best prankster and laugh at everyone who fell for my pranks.

'Wow Dad that was amazing, I need to know how to use this spell.'

'You will son, I will teach you everything I know and you will become even more powerful than me.'

My life was getting very interesting, and I was finally realising that I come from a family that was able to harness the power of magic. This was totally awesome. I looked to the grandfather clock still standing amongst the destruction from the test earlier on and noticed that the day was almost over. Where had time gone, was I really in this test that long or did time go a lot faster in this new magical world I was about to discover. I thought to myself that I would get this Lady Malaga and defeat her once and for all.

'Son I need you to get a good nights sleep tonight, as your training starts tomorrow. Well done today for passing your first test, you will soon know what's real and what's not. We will train and teach you to become the best you can be. Right now you need to be on your guard.' Dad said as he wrapped his arms around me.

Mum clapped her hands and looked over at me and said 'you have done so well today Joe and we are extremely proud of you, you have truly opened your eyes to what is going on around you. Some time very soon you will be stronger than any of us could imagine being.'

With all this chatter from my parents and Uncle Barry, I suddenly knew this was a test and not the dreaded Lady Malaga. This was just a spell to see if I was ready to be taught the next stage of magic. As I walked up the stairs towards my room, I had a feeling of happiness at the prospect of training tomorrow and how much better my life had become. I had a thousand questions running through my head and could not wait to get the answers to all of them. The most important one of all would be what will I be able to do once my training is complete, and if I would be able to make things or myself disappear and then reappear. Roll on tomorrow morning when the training starts.

Chapter 7

TRAINING STARTS

The next morning, I was hoping to wake up with the smell of my Mum cooking breakfast, but this wasn't the case, my bedroom was pitch black and there wasn't any other light in the room. I suddenly thought if I was still in my bedroom at all. I heard a voice say 'Good Morning son, your training starts now.'

What was that supposed to mean and what did I have to do? The voice wasn't giving much away. I asked into the darkness 'What do you mean and what do I have to do?'

The voice replied 'Use your magic to see and not your eyes.'

That's all the information that I got, I was walking around for what felt like the half an hour nearly losing my mind. Suddenly something happened, I cleared my mind and I started to see different colours flick before my eyes. I could only see blurred shapes and objects come into focus, I started to believe this was a test to see what is there and what is not. I focussed more on the blurred shapes and they all started to become clearer. I could make out a light switch on the wall and then a door. I was sure this was my room. I reached over and flipped on the light switch and I was right, this was my bedroom or so I thought. This was a real test and I knew it. I was thinking that I was in my room but I wasn't sure if I was. I looked around to where my bed would have been but I had this strange feeling that it wasn't there. The next instance I could feel an odd heat coming from down by my feet, it was hot coals that lined the floor. I could now understand this test as magic could make me see things that weren't really there. I could hear my Dad's voice again and said 'Well done Son, you have passed your first test, this was one of the most important tests. This spell is called the imagination spell and anyone who can perform magic can use this spell to make things that are not really there appear to play tricks on your mind. This is a very powerful spell and can be used incorrectly if you are not careful.'

I was so pleased with myself that I had passed the first test that had been set and I was sure there was more to come. I was enjoying this new adventure that I was on. I asked Dad if there were more tests just to be sure and my dad laughed and replied 'You're correct in thinking there are more tests to come.'

'Your next test is also so very important and could change your life forever. This spell should only be used as a last resort, this is an example of what could happen so please do not worry or panic.'

Even though my Dad told me not to panic I naturally started to panic, this magic journey I was on was so very cool but also quite scary at the same time. The next spell I was about to see, could mean I could either live in the real world or a made up magical world forever. How long you would be in the made up world would be decided when the spell was cast, this spell was called the Door to Death. Dad could see the worry etched on my face at the name of the spell, and reassured me that the spell got its name because some people have never made it out of the door and have sadly died whilst in the unreal world. Now I understood where this spell got its name from but this did not make it any less scary.

'Right son, I want you to use all your mind strength, don't worry not everyone gets this first time. There will be five doors and the spell will show you your enemies five times, one for each of the doors and all will come with five visions. You have to make a decision to follow them to catch them. Which door are you going to choose to go through? The choice you make will either catch them and where the magic can no longer hurt you, or you go through a door where your enemy is not there and you will be lost in the unreal world for however long.'

There was so much to take in and I didn't know how to reply to my Dad so just said 'ok.' Dad waved his arms in front of him and cast the spell and five doors appeared in front of me. Dad told me to concentrate. I walked up to the first and got a really weird feeling from this door, the second door felt unnaturally cold. The third and fourth doors were warm and boiling hot and finally I got to the fifth and final door and felt nothing from this door at all. This test was really gruelling as I needed to pick the correct door, the first four doors must not be safe to enter as I felt something from all of them. I started to question myself why I couldn't feel anything from the fifth door. I had to make the decision which door I would choose and the silence that had descended around me was making me even more nervous.

I took the plunge and walked up to the door that I thought would not hold my enemies. I grabbed hold of the handle and without warning, the door flung open and pulled me in. It all happened so fast that I could not even get my breath, I couldn't even cry out for help. I was falling and it was reminding me of the time I was falling before. Did everything in the magic world make you feel like you were falling. As I continued my descent, I started to wonder if I had picked the right door after all or would I be stuck here just like my Dad had warned me. I just kept on falling and I began to wonder when all this would end. I must have chosen the wrong door as my gut was telling me this could not be right. Suddenly the bluest sky and the greenest lushest trees came into view and I stopped falling and landed softly on the ground. I looked around and noticed a red door in the distance with a bright red carpet leading up to it. The ground I was on started to move and it made me almost lose my balance. I started to walk towards the door and as I did the further away the door became until it vanished completely. I could see a hill in the distance covered with a dusting of flowers all over it, this wasn't that bad after all but I knew I needed to get out of this magic realm. I suddenly remembered this spell was called the door of death and the only way out would be through the now vanished red door. I had a thought that maybe if I started to explore this realm a little bit the door might reappear for me to use. Maybe this was a test of patience and time and the red door only appears at certain times of the day and that you have to reach this door before this vanishes. I checked my watch and made a note of the time to see if I could pin point when the door disappeared so I would be ready for this when the door reappeared.

I wondered if anyone else was in this world as I would be very lonely if there was nobody else here. Over in the distance I could see something sparkling and could hear the soft trickle of water. This has to lead me somewhere and I'm sure I would discover something to help with rediscovering the red door that would let me leave this realm after all anything was apparently possible with this magical journey i was on. I started to walk towards the hill in the distance and i began to hear a humming in the distance. I kept walking in the direction of the humming and the trickle of water got louder also. I reached the edge of a river and could see the water flowing over some stones on the river bed causing the trickling sound. On the other side of the bank there was a huge oak tree with its branches blowing in the wind, i got closer to have a better look at the tree and realised the humming was coming from the tree itself.

'Wait, who goes there and what are you doing here?' Someone said in an old mans voice.

'I'm Joe, and i am on a test created by my Dad. This is where I ended up, I'm not sure where I am.' I quickly responded.

The tree began to laugh and replied 'A test you say, that's what everyone tells me, I'm afraid I don't believe you.'

I'm so concerned right now, all I could think about was getting out of here and now this tree was standing in my way. The tree was huge and its branches were incredibly long, it could swipe me off my feet in no time at all. I knew i had to play this right, I was busy thinking of what to say when a thought popped into my head and i thought maybe this might just work.

'Yes that's right Mr Tree, I am on a test, I had to pick a door from five different ones to choose from and I ended up here talking to you, I must admit you're a very cool looking tree.' I was hoping that would sweeten up the tree with my compliments. I was giggling inside my head at how stupid this would all sound in my normal life.

'You think you have chosen the correct door do you?' The tree sniggered at me.

'If i am honest with you Mr Tree I'm not entirely sure, what I do know, is that i am so confused right now.'

Suddenly the tree stopped sniggering at me and yelled 'Use your mind lad, use your mind for magic's sake.'

I started to focus and use my mind just like the tree had instructed me to do, I started seeing images of this place and all its wonderful creations and suddenly everything became clearer 'I can see, I really can see now.' I shouted out.

'You can see what lad?' The tree groaned back at me.

I explained to the talking tree that i knew that it was a real tree and that it means me no harm, I also know that you have been here for a very long time and have been watching passers by come and go.

The tree started to howl with laughter and couldn't seem to get its breath, once the laughter had died down and the tree had composed itself it said 'Have you been taking something lad, of course I'm real. I'm a very old tree who has been here for hundreds of years. This place used to be filled with all my family and friends trees and over the years I've watched on as they have been taken away from me and i am now the only one left. I'm Sir George, the famous happy singing tree.'

'Nice to meet you Sir George, can I ask where your friends and family have gone?'

'She has taken them, the witch!' Sir George replied.

'You mean Lady Malaga?'

'Yes the witch, she cast a spell on them to leave here and become her servants and do as she wanted them to do. They were once very friendly, but have now fallen under her spell and are fully controlled by her.'

'Thats awful I'm so sorry, is there anything that i would be able to do to help get your friends and family back?'

'Help? You're just a boy, there is nothing you can do. Just look at you, you wouldn't stand a chance against her, no offence meant by that.' Sir George replied.

'You couldn't offend me so none taken, I am in training so one day I'll face her and stop her.'

'Good luck lad, you are going to need it.'

I didn't know how to reply to Sir George's last statement as i knew deep down that he was right and i was just a young boy. I knew i would become more than this in order to face Lady Malaga and defeat her. Sir George had lit a fire in my belly and this urged me to want to do this more than ever now. I asked Sir George what the red door was as he must of seen this in the many years that he had lived here and he told me that this was my way out of this realm. He also explained that i needed to be very quick to be able to catch the door and that he didn't think i was quite ready to face the challenge of the red door. I knew deep down that i might be stuck here for quite a while and then Sir George echoed my feelings, it felt like he had looked into my thoughts and spoke exactly what i was thinking. Sir George went on to offer me some tips and tricks to help on my conquest to catch the red door.

That sounded like a great plan but i knew i needed to be getting back to Uncle Barry's house and for my other tests to continue. I remembered my Dad saying this was just a practice test and i thought that if I didn't reach the door in time, he would come and get me from here. I began to hope so even though i had started to really like Sir George and his lovely woody heart, he was not that scary after all, lets just hope he had complete control of his branches. I tried to keep the chuckle inside but a small chuckle escaped from within me because i could not get over that i was talking to a tree.

I asked Sir George what he was going to show me and he explained that he too knew some magic and could make different objects appear. Within seconds a shining golden box appeared in the distance, it looked so far away from where i was currently standing but i was ready. Sir George explained that he would give me ten minutes to reach the box and told me to act like the box was the red door that i needed to reach to make it back home.

I was ready for this challenge and egged myself on in my head, I started running towards the golden box and as I inched closer and closer towards the box, it became clearer. I must have been running for around eight minutes when the box started to fade away, I had a split second thought that I was not going to reach the box in time, but I shook that thought away as soon as it entered my mind. I was not going to lose this box, I willed myself to reach the box before it disappeared. I reached deep into my mind and hoped that I would make it. Within seconds my feet lifted off the ground and I was moving faster and faster, getting closer and closer towards the box it felt like I was flying through the air. Suddenly my feet dropped back to the ground and right in front of me was the box. I didn't understood how this had happened but anything that seemed abnormal to me was obviously the normal in this new life I was living. I grabbed for the box just before it disappeared just like the red door, I then looked back towards Sir George but all of a sudden I was standing right next to him.

'You've only gone and done it, I don't believe it, you going to be the one to save us all.' Sir George exclaimed!

I needed to sit down as I could not believe I had completed Sir George's mini test on my first attempt, what had just happened and did I really float through the air? I knew I had made it as I was back next to Sir George. He went on to explain that I was the one they had all been waiting for, waiting for so many years and nothing had happened. Many had attempted Sir George's golden box test but so many had failed. Sir George went on to explain that he had been waiting to meet the one who could pass his test and that I had a lot more to learn and that he had great faith in me and my abilities. He explained that he had the power to make anyone stay here indefinitely or grant them permission to leave this realm. When the curse is cast, it all depends on the person who comes through the door and what happens to them, if they don't pass the test, they either stay here indefinitely or I send them to another world that has stricter and more far wide consequences. As you are the only one to have completed my test and I can sense you come from a good place, I grant you permission to leave but mark my words lad, we will meet again.

Before I had the chance to say goodbye to Sir George a bright light sparkled from my feet and before I knew it I was back outside the red door, I glanced back towards Sir George and i could just make out the smile of his bark and his branches waving wildly in the wind, I grabbed the handle of the door and pulled it open, I peered inside and could see my parents looking at me with the biggest grins on their faces. Suddenly the door started to pull me back into my own world.

'Well how was it Joe?' Mum asked

'Oh my god, I met a lovely.'

'Don't say it, Sir George am I right?' Mum interrupted.

'Yes that's right, have you met him before Mum?'

'We all met the lovely Sir George, he helped us all so much, but that is not always the case with everyone.'

'I guessed that, but I have really enjoyed my day learning all I have learnt.'

'You are not done yet Joe' I looked at my Mum in complete shock

'Close your mouth Joe, there is lots you need to learn. In this lesson you will learn the ability to talk to all trees like Sir George. There are some that are not so friendly, this is why you will be learning to know which ones you should and shouldn't talk to.'

I shouted out in excitement because I had loved my time with Sir George and his comical ways.

'I can't wait to tell my friends and show them all my new powers and what I can do with them.' I said to my parents.

'You can never show anyone your powers Joe except those people who you know are the same as you.' Mum shouted back at me.

'Sorry Mum, this is all just new and so exciting, I will promise I will keep it to myself, but how do I tell who else is like me?'

Mum explained that it would come to me in time. As I am shown more and complete more tests it will become natural to know who else is just like me. She said that there is a sign in the eyes of the people who possess magic. She told me that I would need to look very closely at her eyes and I would see a yellow dot in the centre and that i should also hold this sign. I looked very closely and carefully into my Mums eyes and just like she said there was a yellow dot. I quickly turned to the mirror to look into my eyes as I had never noticed a yellow dot before. The more I looked into my eyes the clearer I could see my own yellow dot. I dashed over to my Dad to see if he also had the secret yellow dot in his eyes and he did. This was the sign that we were all the same and all possessed the power that came with magic.

'There you go Joe, that was another lesson for you, how to identify someone who is the same as you.'

'Ok, I have another question. I know I have the yellow dot, does that mean Lady Malaga does to?'

'She did have many years ago, the yellow dot means good magic, we are called the yellows. now that she has turned evil, she will have a red dot. These are known as the reds. There are also the blues, a blue dot in your eye would mean you are being controlled by one of the reds. We understand this is a lot to take in, but you will learn. This is how we can detect if the person you are facing is kind, evil, or controlled.'

That made sense, now I would know which kind of person I was facing. Mum went on to say that she needed to show me about the trees and that we were getting side tracked.

Dad was so quiet but I think he was secretly impressed with Mum talking me though everything. Mum knew the time had come for her to train up her son and to get me prepared for what was coming.

Mum held out her hand and muttered under her breath 'Yellow, show yourself.'

Suddenly a yellow ring appeared on her finger, I had never seen anything like this before. It was big and ornate and looked like it belonged in a time from many years ago. I gasped and wondered to myself where it had come from. Mum explained that the ring is used to cast any magic and that the caster must have activated their own yellow ring. All the casters magic is held within their rings and if they didn't have their rings they would have no magic at all. Mum asked if I had noticed all the tiny little yellow stones that decorated the edge of the ring. I knew that was what had caught my eye and looked at them more carefully. Mum told me that after you pass a magic test, your ring gets rewarded with a magic stone. There are forty spaces for forty magic stones in total so I gathered I must have to pass forty tests. There are two types of yellows, the ones who pass all the tests and have been awarded with all forty stones and those who cannot pass all the tests and will not be as powerful as those with all forty stones. I knew there was so much to learn and I knew this would take time.

'This sounds so good, have I got a yellow ring now?'
I asked my Mum.

'Once you have completed your first cast, you will feel the ring appear under your finger, this isn't very nice at first. You will get used to it, it's like a toothache at first, but this will get easier the more you cast and practice. Like I said to you before, what I will teach you will change your life forever, but I believe you are ready.'

That sounds horribly painful as I could remember from having toothaches in the past and was not looking forward to feeling this pain again but I was so ready for my first cast. Mum explained that she was about to cast a spell and that I needed to hold on to her tightly and that we were going to a safe place to practice. Mum raised her hand and started to cast, instantly the room began to spin, it was spinning so fast that I felt like I was on a fair ride and that I could be sick at any minute. Mum shouted at me to hold on tight and to not let her go. I did as I was told and held on tight, the room was still spinning and through the haze created by the spin I could start to see field upon field of lush green grass.

'You made it son, at first I thought you might have let go.' Mum said with a laugh.

I asked my Mum what this place was and where we were and Mum replied that we were in a safe place where all the yellows can practice their magic ahead of their magical tests. I went on to ask about the tests and what they consisted of and who did the tests but all Mum said was that she would tell me when I was ready. She explained it was time for my first test and to see if I could achieve my first yellow stone for my ring. I started to think of how I would get my ring and if it would hurt as much as Mum told me it would.

I couldn't wait to get my first yellow stone as this meant that all this was not a dream and I was actually living in the magical world. How could this all have been within my family and I never knew anything about it. Mum told me to get ready and I mentally prepared myself for my first test. Mum raised her hands in front of her and started to cast a spell. In front of my eyes trees started to appear out of nowhere. There must have been at least ten trees all around me with more appearing as the seconds ticked by. The trees were all different shapes and sizes and many different types of trees. Some had happy expressions on their barks whilst others looked damn right evil. I didn't fully understand what was expected of me or what I should do. Trees now surrounded me on all sides and I could not see my Mum anymore, more and more trees started to appear with no signs of stopping anytime soon. All I could see were the eyes of the trees baring down on me, suddenly I heard my Mums voice through the gaps of the trees and she said 'Joe, this is your test to identify which trees are nice and which ones are evil, you will need to make quick decisions. This could change your life as the reds can use these as weapons, so you will have to be quick. The evil trees won't be so nice, they will use their branches against you, they will throw out their smaller branches towards you like knives. You will need to cast a protection spell around yourself to stop you getting hurt from these branches.'

Now I started to feel fear in the pit of my stomach as this magic business was no joke, I knew that if i followed my Mum's instructions to the letter I should be ok. I asked my Mum where my ring was was as I knew I needed to cast the protection spell to keep me safe. Mum explained how I would get my ring and what words I needed to say to activate my ring. You need to raise your hand over the other and say 'Awaken ring, I am ready, set the first test.' It is important to get these words right, I know you will feel pain like i explained but this is the only way to make your ring active.

I explained to my Mum that I was scared but she reassured me that I would be fine and that she believed in me. I knew I had to make my Mum proud and I knew this was time to get ready for my life to change forever.

I did as my Mum explained and raised one hand over the other and spoke out the words that were needed to activate my own ring.

'Awaken ring, I am ready, set the first test.'

My hands started to shake and I could feel a burning sensation pass through my hands and down my fingers. The trees started moving in on me and I knew this was going to get bad. I looked down at my ring finger and noticed it start to go yellow. It felt like my finger was going to drop off at any point. Suddenly the burning stopped and the shaking of my hands started to calm down.

'Joe can you see your yellow ring, it may be faint, but if you can see it, you are ready to cast the spell to protect yourself?' I heard my Mum say.

I excitedly told my Mum that I could see a slight yellow mark on my finger and she exclaimed that this was great. I was told the words to say that would have protected me from the impeding tree attack. *Yellow Strong, Yellow Protect.*

I could see that the trees were not going to wait much longer and some of them started to angrily raise their branches. I raised my ring hand and shouted out the words my Mum had told me to say just in time. *Yellow Strong, Yellow Protect.*

Suddenly a yellow bubble appeared in thin air and then wrapped itself around my body, this was just in time as a branch was launched at me and more were coming my way. I told my Mum what had happened and she said that I had done great and that I was in the first test.

Mum told me how the test would work ' I need you to identify the good and bad trees now, you will have to walk up to the trees and place your hand on the trees. When you do this you will feel the power flow into your ring and award you your first stone. You need to get through the evil trees before you can reach the good ones. Remember to look the trees dead set in the eyes and you have fifteen minutes to complete this test, good luck.'

I was so ready for this and I had my hands on my knees bent over like I was getting ready to run a marathon. I could hear my Mum cry out, 'Get Ready, Set, Go.' Suddenly the trees started to come at me really fast, I dodged out of the way but these trees were quick but I knew the protection spell would keep me safe. I moved out of the way from a few more evil trees and I could sense they were not happy. They threw their branches at me like I was a dart board, suddenly I realised there was a slight hole in my protection bubble. I asked out to my Mum what I was to do as I thought this was going to keep me safe. My Mum explained to me that this would only give me a certain amount of protection and the idea of the spell was to offer me slight protection but I needed to be quicker with my enemies. She asked if I thought this test was going to be that easy and I replied no, but I'm only young and don't want to die just yet.

Mum explained I would not die but I better keep dodging the trees that were firing out the branches towards me and that I would be able to run between them to get to the good trees behind the evil ones. All I could see at the minute were evil trees and I knew they were as their eyes were filled with hatred and had turned a red colour instead of the usual yellow. I heard my Mum shouted for me to concentrate and to remember what I had been taught already. I thought I would not pass this test and all I could see were red eyes everywhere, I couldn't see any yellow eyes of the good trees anywhere. The evil trees started to get more aggressive towards me. I noticed a particularly large evil tree that was continually firing tree spikes towards me and I knew my protection bubble was not going to hold much longer.

I shouted out to my Mum that nothing was working and I was scared that my protection was not going to last. There were too many evil trees around me. I screamed out for her to help me. I fell to the ground and the trees started moving closer and closer. I tried to move my legs and noticed that I could not feel them let alone move them. Suddenly I felt a tree spike pierce through my leg and I cried out in pain, I knew I was doomed and started to wonder why my mum would leave me here with no help at all. I cried out for her again but there was no sign of her. I closed my eyes and wished that I could leave this place, and that the trees would leave me alone. I wished this would work and wondered if my Mum knew I was in trouble. Suddenly the trees were blasted from around me and flew to the other edge of the field I was in. Mum ran up to me and looked worried, I knew now this was not how this test was meant to go.

'Quick Joe we have to run, hurry up and move come on!' Mum shouted

'Mum I can't move my leg, it's been injured, this was such a bad idea, I wasn't ready.' I replied

'Joe we have to go, I can't stop them either!' Mum cried at me

'What do you mean you can't stop them? You were the one who cast them here.'

'There is someone else controlling them, I have lost control, I can't stop them at all, this magic's power is too strong. I'm sorry Joe, this wasn't meant to happen, we should of been safe here. Someone has set a trap here but I need us to get out of here right now.'

'Where can we go? There is nowhere to go, can't you use your magic to get us back home?'

'Joe watch out!' I heard Mum scream out

There she was standing in front of her tree army, and my Mum looked so helpless.

I heard my Mum shout out at her to take her instead and to leave me alone.

Chapter 8

SHES BACK

I could feel my body being lifted up from the ground and could hear evil laughter fill the air. I looked at my Mum in the distance and noticed her watching in horror. What was going on made no sense at all. I heard my Mum shout out and I finally realised that I had been captured floating through the air getting higher and higher from the ground. I suddenly felt a force pulling me back towards the ground and noticed a yellow glow around my legs and I knew this was my Mum trying to save me. I knew this was no good as the laughter in the background was getting louder and louder. I suddenly started to fall to the ground and during my descent I watched my Mum run towards me. She caught a spell that would have broken my fall and caught me before my face had smashed into the ground. I watched as my Mum made several attempts but this was no good as Lady Malaga's magic was just so powerful and was wiping away my Mums attempts at creating a protection spell.

I heard Lady Malaga shout out 'You can have your boy back for now, but you know you cant keep him from me forever. He will be mine, there is no point in kidding yourself.' She laughed most wickedly. With a flick of her wrist I was released from her spell that was keeping me prisoner.

'Joe I got you!' I heard my Mum shout as she cast out again to catch my fall.

I looked over to Lady Malaga and saw she was floating in the air, a cloud of black magic around her. I looked at her eyes and could see that they were all red exactly like I was told to expect from all those who were evil. They seemed to pierce right through me and knew that she was pure evil, the power that was flowing around her was something else, I started to think how I would face her when I was ready as I thought that she was far too powerful.

'You think you can stop me do you, I'll show you what true power is.' I heard Lady Malaga scream at us.

The black cloud of magic that was covering Lady Malaga seem to come alive and a burst of red lightening shot out of her. It crackled as it flew through the air and hit the ground. As it hit the ground, the force of the magic made us both fall to our knees.

I heard Lady Malaga shout 'You will both be challenged now. Will your Mummy be able to keep you safe, I'm sure we are about to find out.' She cackled with evil laughter.

Another shot of red lightening flew out from her and struck all of her trees. The trees shook as the lightening hit and this looked like this was making them more powerful. I looked over towards my Mum and she looked terrified that she would not be able to stop them. I shouted out for my Mum to watch out and more bolts of red lightening kept coming at us at full speed. Suddenly the bolts of lightening changed to red powerful flames, I knew we didn't stand a chance. Mum was trying her best to stop the bolts of lightening and fire hitting us by casting back towards them. I could feel my Mums energy starting to fall and could see she was getting so very tired and I knew this could be the point we were done for.

I heard Lady Malaga cackle in the background and said 'Hand me the boy and you can live or you will die trying to save him.'

My Mum shouted back at her 'never' and I watched as my Mum cast out with the energy that she had left. This time the magic that come from my Mum was so bright and powerful and she had aimed it directly at Lady Malaga. She was caught off guard and my Mums spell hit the black cloud of magic that surrounded Lady Malaga. I looked over to my Mum and then back at Lady Malaga and could see her falling to the ground. Mum grabbed hold of me and then cast a spell, the light surrounded us and I knew we were travelling back to safety. I didn't see if Lady Malaga had hit the ground as we were transported back.

We ended up back in the garden of Uncle Barry's house and collapsed onto the ground. That had been a frightening experience and we had come so close to Lady Malaga capturing me for good. Her magic was just so strong, I didn't know how we would stop her and if I was strong enough to face her again. Dad and Barry ran out into the garden and stopped in front of us. I turned to my Mum and asked if she was ok and said we had a close call. She did not say anything back to me.

'Where have you been? You have been ages, how did Joe get on? Did you pass the first test?' Dad asked Mum and I.

I heard my Mum say to my Dad that she needed to lay down. Barry looked at me and asked what I have been up to, Mum shook her head and I took this as she didn't want me to say anything, I guess Mum will explain everything later on. I looked over at my Uncle and told him that I also needed a lie down. I heard my Uncle talking to my Dad as Mum and I walked towards the house. That we both needed a lie down after all todays training and that he would wait to hear about it all later on when we are both refreshed and rested.

I heard my Dad say that he would get dinner sorted for us all while we were resting and I said thank you to Dad and told my Mum that would be great and didn't hear a reply from her. I think all her energy has been used up with all the casting she had done to save me from the grasps of Lady Malaga. I decided to leave my Mum to rest and knew that she would be a lot better later on after a rest. I walked towards my bedroom and could see my bedroom door open, this was odd as I always closed my bedroom door. I slowly walked towards my door and it slightly opened a little bit more, I did not want to bother my Mum again and knew I had to deal with this myself. I had learnt a lot today so I knew I could cope with anything at this point. I swung open my door and shouted out that I was ready to whoever was in my room. I heard nothing back and as I entered my bedroom there was the same black cat digging its claws into my favourite pillow on my bed.

'What you doing here cat? What do you want?' I asked the cat.

'I heard you were in a slight bit of trouble earlier Joe, I came to see if you made it back home, and here you are right as rain,' exclaimed the cat

I explained to the cat, that I was indeed back and that I didn't want to sound rude but I needed to rest after what had happened today. The cat looked offended and told me he knew when he was not wanted. The cat leapt onto the window frame and out of the window. I started to feel bad with how abrupt I was but I just needed to rest. The cat would come back and speak to me I was sure of it, I suddenly thought I did not know the cats name. I made a mental note to ask his name the next time he showed up again. I was so pleased to see my bed and regardless of the shredded pillow I collapsed onto it and fell asleep with exhaustion. I was asleep for a few hours and just as I was waking up slowly and opening my eyes I could see a figure in front of me and jumped out of my skin. I willed my eyes to wake up quicker and hastily found that I was looking at my Mum, she was just standing there staring at me and not saying a word. This was not like my Mum at all, she suddenly said that dinner was ready and slowly walked out of my room.

Mum was not acting like herself at all and I didn't know I should say anything as I did not want to upset anyone. I thought I would talk to Dad later on to see if he had noticed anything different in Mum's behaviour. I would also need to find out if Mum had told Dad everything that had happened today. I thought back to Mum and put it down to all the magic she had cast today and thought that it had truly drained the energy out of her. I called out to ask Mum if she was coming downstairs for dinner and I got no response at all. I heard her slam the bedroom door. Uncle Barry shouted up the stairs to stop slamming doors in his house, I shouted back down that it was me and the wind had caught the door and apologised. I would let Mum rest and tomorrow she would be back to normal. Uncle Barry told me to come down for dinner and wake my Mum up on the way. There was no way I was waking her up and facing her anger for being disturbed again.

As I made my way down the stairs I could feel someone watching me, I turned and looked up the stairs and I could not believe that Mum, was standing there staring at me like she was when she was back in my bedroom. I started to think if this was really my Mum, I remembered being told to check someone's eyes to give me a sign of who they were. I tried to do this with Mum but the light in the hallway was too dark and dingy to make out any colour in her eyes. I turned back around to make my way down the last few stairs and suddenly there was a rush of air from behind me like someone was running down the stairs. Within seconds Mum was behind me as I could feel her breath on the back of my neck, how the hell did she get behind me so fast. I now knew this wasn't my Mum and someone must be controlling her. I made a bolt into the kitchen and in my craze I nearly slid into my Dad and Uncle Barry. I shouted out that there was something wrong with Mum and that they needed to do something. Dad turned round in a shocked rage and Barry looked like he was laughing. They both asked what i meant and I explained that Mum was acting really weird. Dad said that I was starting to scare him and demanded I tell him everything that had happened today.

'I wasn't going to say anything, I was going to let Mum tell you Dad.'

'Tell me what!' Dad shouted at me

'Ummmmm.'

'Stop ummmming and tell me will you.' Dad exclaimed.

I could tell Dad was not happy at all, as he had started to shout at me and his face had a slight tinge of pink in the cheeks like he always did when he was angry.

'Well the training didn't go as Mum planned, there were some trees and Lady.' Before I could finish of what I was saying, Dad shouted out to me and said why didn't i tell him something as important as Lady Malaga?

'I'm sorry Dad, Mum didn't look at all happy when I was going to say something earlier on.'

Dad asked if I had seen the colour of my Mum's eyes and I paused before I answered him. Dad shouted at me to give him an answer and I explained that it was too dark upstairs to make any colours out in my eyes. He demanded that I stay in the kitchen and not to go anywhere else. I could see that something was not right and it was written all over my Dad's face. What had happened to my Mum was the only question running through my head right now. I heard my Dad run up the stairs and Uncle Barry followed after him. I heard Uncle Barry say to my Dad that he knew this would happen and that he hoped it was not too late. Too late for what I questioned in my head? What the hell was happening or what could have happened to get this reaction from both of them and for my Mum to be acting so strange. I heard my Dad banging around upstairs searching every room for Mum as he went from room to room I knew that he could not find her. I sat waiting patiently for them both to return. I looked out of the kitchen window and could see a figure outside. I went over to the window to get a better look and could see that Mum was walking around outside. I called up to my Dad and Uncle Barry and told them that Mum was outside. As Dad and Uncle Barry ran down the stairs, Dad said to Uncle Barry to watch me and look after me. Why I wouldn't be safe was beyond me as this was only Mum. Dad threw open the back door and shouted out, 'I know this isn't you, let her go now.'

I ran towards the back door and looked out into the garden and could see Mum and Dad facing off with each other. Suddenly Mum lifted herself off the ground and started to float up into the sky, she tilted her head back and shouted out 'Oh how I have missed this.' Abruptly Mum flung her arms open and a bolt of lightening shot out from her and made contact with the ground. As it hit the ground there was an almighty crack as the ground started to split. I now knew this wasn't my Mum but the dreaded Lady Malaga. How had she come back with us earlier on and what had she done with my mother. Dad shouted for everyone to get back and with this the laughter began echoing across the sky.

'You think you can defeat me, poor Stella is now trapped and only I can control her, stay back or I will drop her to her death. You know what I want and I will not stop at anything until I get what I want. I will give you a day to make your mind up, Catch.'

With this Lady Malaga left my Mum's body and Mum started to fall towards the ground, Dad kept over the crack in the ground to catch Mum and only just made it. Mum landed in Dad's arms and Mum's eyes flung open 'What's going on and where am I, why the hell am I outside?' Mum says in a groggy sleepy voice.

Dad speaks to Mum 'It's ok, I've got you now, we need to talk about earlier on, but first let me get you inside.'

Lady Malaga was not going to give up, she really did want me and will try her hand at anything to get me. I knew we would have to come up with a plan as I was not ready to face her as I had not passed any of my tests and I knew the ring would not be at its full power and neither would I. Dad asked me to go inside with them all, we made our way into the front room and sat around each other on the sofas just looking at each other. It was Dad who was the first to speak out.

'Ok, this is no laughing matter, now she is back and means business, we have been given a day to think of a plan. She won't stop this time, she has given us a choice to make.'

Mum looked over to Dad and asked 'what do you mean we have a choice to make?' Dad explained that Mum would not have remembered that Lady Malaga took over your body and you were lifted from the ground and you started to attack us. Dad started to laugh as Mum's face looks horrified.

'Lightening bolts I'm sorry.' Mum laughs back.

'It's ok I knew it wasn't you.' Dad smirks.

How can my parents be joking with each other right now with everything that is going on, I am in a total state of shock. I ask both my parents to stop joking as this was all about me and I was the one she was after. My Dad apologised and said that they all make jokes to calm the situation down. Uncle Barry walked into the room with a pot of tea and asked who wants a cup. Mum and Dad both said yes please and I just shake my head at him. Uncle Barry shouts is that a yes or no, I reply 'yes please.' Somehow a pot of tea in these situations always helps. I knew I had to pluck up the courage to ask both my Mum and Dad why Lady Malaga wanted me so much and what did she want from me.

'Dad, why does Lady Malaga want me so much?'

'Son I knew this time would come, your mum and I knew this and wished every day it would never be the day, we do need to tell you more, so you understand completely. We were told when you were born you were very special, that you could change the world. I know this sounds very odd to you son, but it's true, you will have a great power. Your not ready to use that power just yet but once you have fully trained you will become unstoppable.'

'Jake I think we need to tell Joe, why she wants our son.'

Mum replies.

Chapter 9

DAD EXPLAINS

Dad explains that he knew Uncle Barry had told me a great deal of stuff and that he also gave me some tea that allowed me to see into the past and said he wasn't happy at first with this decision. I knew you would have to go on this journey but I was upset that I wasn't here with you to help you through that experience. Your Mum was here so that put my mind at rest a little bit. He went on to explain that I needed to know so much more and I he knew about Uncle Barry's plan to make some more yellow tea after the accident you had with the last batch. I'm so glad I'm here for you now and also I'm glad you didn't use the yellow tea as this could be so dangerous if you used this on your own. I explained to Dad what happened with the first batch of tea and also how the cat knocked it over.

Dad told me to get comfortable and to drink my tea before it went cold and explained we were going back at least one hundred years. I know you have seen into Lady Malaga's past and what happened to her Mum. Uncle Barry must have told my Dad everything we had already been through and about the young man who was into magic, but he was so different to all of us.

'Different in what way?' I asked my Dad.

'Let me finish son, please don't be so impatient, all will make sense shortly.'

Mum then told Dad off for repeating himself and Dad became angry and shouted out 'Can you all please just let me finish.'

I looked over at my Mum and she gave me a sly smile, this made me think she was making a joke out of my Dad.

Dad continued with what he was telling us.

There was a young man who was fascinated with magic and loved to experiment and create his own spells. The young man was obsessed with all living creatures, even those down to the smallest fly. The thought of any creature dying filled the man's heart with sadness. He tried to help in all ways he could and tried to create a spell that could bring things back from the brink of death. He was a very lonely young man and had to remember that practicing magic held a death sentence in the human world. He obviously came from a magical background and his parents were hardly ever around. His parents where always away fighting to keep the family fed. In their small house lived his Mum, Dad, Grandpa and him.

As his parents were always away it was down to the young man's Grandpa to look after him. During the time they spent together, his Grandpa would show him a few select spells and the young man was fascinated with everything that he was shown. As the years passed the young man was taught everything the Grandpa knew. I asked my Dad if the Grandpa was a witch as he had the use of magic and my Dad laughed and said he supposed we called him a wizard.

Dad went on to explain that the Grandpa was called Walter and the young man's Father was called William and his Mum was called Cordelia. His Mum did not appreciate magic and detested it with every fibre of her being. She would not allow it in the house at all, so the Grandpa created a magical workshop where Walter could show the young man all of his magic. I asked my Dad what the young man was called and Dad told me he was also called Joe. This was so exciting as he shared my name. Dad went on to explain that this was actually me from a past life and I could not believe what was coming from my Dad's mouth. Dad told me that he was going to continue what he was saying and then I would be able to ask any questions at the end.

Dad went back to his tale and the magic workshop where the Joe from the past would learn all manner of magical things from his Grandad. Even when his Grandpa was not there Joe would spend all day and night practicing magic, trying to experiment and create a spell that would harness the power of life. One day he succeeded and created the spell of life.

From the moment the spell was created everything changed. Joe was so very pleased with himself with what he had achieved. He was so excited that he wanted to show his Grandpa Walter. He found a bird that had sadly passed away and brought it into the magical workshop. His Grandpa could not believe what his Grandson was telling him but went along with what Joe was so excited with. Joe cast a spell on the dead bird and suddenly the bird started to move and then its wings started to unfurl as life was restored to the bird. Walter looked over in horror and knew that Joe had created a spell that could be used as an evil weapon. Walter cast a spell over the bird to remove Joe's magic and the bird turned to black ash. Joe looked distraught and Walter knew he had to act immediately. He knew he could not let Joe cast this spell again or even remember anything he had ever shown Joe. He knew Joe could be a dangerous person to be around and this spell could make him a lot of friends that would be unwanted and looking to use Joe instead of being his true friend. Walter cast a spell of forgetfulness over Joe to wipe away Joe's magic for the next one hundred years. He knew this spell only had this amount of time before it stopped working and dreaded the day the spell would break. Walter had a funny feeling in his stomach that someone or something had seen this spell and knew what had happened.

After this I asked my Dad what had happened and Dad continued with the story. Walter knew that he had to do something to protect Joe and get him as far away as possible but this was too late. There was a bang at the door and the door was thrown open. It was a young Lady Malaga and her mother. They wanted to become friends with Joe and Walter but with an alternative motif in mind. Lady Malaga's mother knew she had to make Joe remember the magic he had learnt and also the spell that he had created. She attempted to break the curse Walter had cast over Joe but this magic was too strong to be broken. So in order to get her own way she cast a counter curse over Joe that would make his soul live on forever and pass down to every male heir in the Walters family. This way when the time was right Lady Malaga could get her own way and reveal the spell that would change the whole world for the better or so she thought.

I asked my Dad why she was after me and Dad told me that I had a very old soul and I was one of those in the generation that this curse was cast upon. I had the spell trapped within my mind, but I would not remember it until Walter's original curse started to break. I still didn't understand why she would want me, I didn't remember the spell. Dad continued to say that she would make me remember and break

Walter's curse and she needs this one spell to make her the most powerful being and take over the world.

I was told she had been trying for so long to get to me but she was never strong enough before but something changed when the current me was born. Your Mum and I have tried our best to keep you away from all of this and to keep you growing up as normal as we could. Dad explained that there was only so much they could do and knew the time was coming when they could not hold me back anymore as the time was coming that Walter's curse would break. I was told that she would be coming back for me but it was only me who could change everything and when she did come back it would only be me who could make the decision on what to do. I asked my Dad what the hell he was on about and Mum shouted at my Dad not to scare me, she told me that she would not hurt me but needed me and wanted to train me up in her ways of magic. I thought out loud and said she may as well take me then, if she was not going her hurt me I would be safe. It was the only way she would get this spell but also the only way I would remember the lessons the past me was taught.

Mum told me that it was my choice but that they didn't know what she would do in time to be able to get the spell but this would be the best chance I had to make my fight against her. Mum also explained that she would train me in all ways magical and that my yellow ring would not be yellow anymore but this would turn red and that I would become her apprentice. Dad went on to explain that they both love me so very much but there could be a chance I would change sides and that if I ever did, even my parents would turn against me and have to battle me. I told them both that would never happen and I would never do anything to jeopardise or harm my parents. I was told her magic was very powerful and that both my parents were so worried that this day would come and had tried to give me the best childhood that they could away from this life. Uncle Barry explained this was why he pushed me to look into the past to see if I would remember anything.

As you could imagine a million thoughts were flying through my head. Would I let her take me or should I stand and fight. If I was going to stand and fight I thought this would be a little too unpractical as I didn't know much magic. I made a split decision to let her take me and train me up, once she had done this I could stand and fight to be able to take her down once and for all.

'Ok, I think Joe has heard enough now, can we all just stop this. We only have a day left before she returns, I want us all to have a happy time please. Joe no harm will come to you.' Mum said.

'It's ok Mum I understand, I'm ready to face what is coming. At first this was all strange and scary to me, but I now know what I have to do. Like you both said I hold something so powerful inside me and I'm ready to learn everything, it's just a shame I cant do it with you and Dad.'

'My brave boy you will be stronger than all of us, I don't know how long it will take you Joe but I know you will be back, you're strong, brave and powerful. We love you so very much.'

We all stood and hugged each other and Mum leaked a few tears of sadness but we all knew this was a decision we had to stand by. The silence that had descended over the house was pierced with an evil cackling laughter that we knew belonged to none other than Lady Malaga.

'How sweet this is, I must admit it's touched my dark black heart I must say.'

All of our heads spun around and there in front of the fire place was the person we all dreaded the arrival of, our day was not over and I began to wonder what the hell she was doing here already.

'I haven't come to cause any of you any trouble for a change. I will keep my promise, you still have a day, I've come to leave Joe a little present.'

She raised her hand and started to cast a spell and out of nowhere a black door started to materialise out of thin air. The door was a much bigger one than any usual door and was decorated with ornate markings and cracks. My eyes were drawn to the large handle that was fixed on one side, it was an eerily red colour and shining like it had its own life force.

'Once your day is over boy, the door will open and you must walk through it alone. Do not forget to say your goodbyes. Oh a word of warning to you all, do not let anyone else but Joe open the door or cast your feeble attempts of magic on my creation as I will know. This has been written and you cannot change what is meant to be.' With a cackle of her laughter she vanished.

Dad suddenly come up with an idea as to how we could get around the predicament we were in, he explained it was risky but that it could work. He asked my Mum if she remembered the time when they cast a cloning spell, to clone my Dad to see if anyone would notice any difference, this was for a time when my Dad was unwell. My Mum said she remembered very well and Uncle Barry spoke out and said how ace the magic was but it did take them almost a day to do and that it could work in this situation.

So they were all thinking of making another version of me. They were trying to play Lady Malaga at her own games of manipulation. Dad explained that this could work but this would take the whole evening and even halfway through the next day. He also said they could cast a spell of secrecy to stop Lady Malaga knowing what they were up to but said that she could not return until the day was over but needed to hurry and get on with their mission. Everyone agreed and then they all turned to me and looked for my reaction and answer. I said 'yes' I was happy with the plan but had some doubts as to whether this would work. Uncle Barry started to laugh and said to me 'You have no clue what us three can do when we work together.'

Dad called everyone into action and asked Uncle Barry to get an old green bucket, I looked over at my Dad and he started to laugh. The green bucket is a magical bucket where we can make spells, so if something went wrong, the bucket would withstand the magic and contain the spell within. Uncle Barry runs away to go and hunt for the bucket and Dad turned to Mum and asked her why she looked so unhappy, she told my Dad she was fine but just a little bit worried. Dad reassured Mum and said that we needed to do something and if this could trick Lady Malaga, we could possibly get away with it for a week or two. In that time we could teach Joe all the magic we know and then he would be ready to take her on. Mum finally agreed with Dad's plan and Dad shouted out to see where Uncle Barry had got to. Just as Dad finished shouting, Uncle Barry ran back into the living room. I watched as they all stood around the bucket and started to cast spells. I looked over to the bucket and could not believe my eyes, from within the bucket, I could see a figure starting to form very slowly. This was totally amazing. Dad shouted out that he needed a light spell and Mum cast it straight away, Dad explained that this was to make sure the clone would not be able to do anything evil just good deeds.

Spells shot from all of their hands and they were all muttering so many words that I could not make out any of them. I could see the spells starting to work as the shape from within the bucket was starting to form a pair of legs. It looked so very odd but the good thing was that it was working. I looked up at the clock and could see that they had all been working for the last three hours, where had the time gone, I did not know. All three of them looked exhausted and that the shadow of sleep could fall over them at any point. I was very grateful to them allfor their efforts to save me. I called out to them to see if I could do anything to help but it was like they were in a trance like state, I knew when they started casting this complex magic they would not be able to stop. I sat around for a few more hours watching how cool all three of them looked while doing some incredible magic. The clone of me was now looking exactly like me and was coming together really well, I laughed inside my head as I thought of which one was better looking. I suddenly remembered the sweets Mum brought with us to Uncle Barry's house and went off to find them as they were my favourite Lemon Sherbets. I got back into the living room with a pocket full of my sweets and could see something was happening with my clone. It was moving its arm and life started to flow through the creation. This was incredible how it could go from being an empty green bucket to a human clone of myself, if you could call it a human.

Uncle Barry walked away from the circle and looking exhausted he looked at me and said 'That's all I can do, my body is exhausted and can do no more, it's down to your parents to finish now.'

I replied to him 'Uncle Barry, I can't believe this would really work, he looks so real.'

Uncle Barry warned me not to get too close to my clone as he was a replacement to bide us more time to get me ready to possibly defeat Lady Malaga. I didn't want to know what she would do when she finally realised that we had tricked her. This sent shivers down my spine as my Uncle was right, my clone would be in mortal danger when she found out, but the subconscious said it would be fine as he was just a spell. I asked my Uncle if this was correct and Uncle Barry explained that yes he was just a spell, but as time went on, the clone would develop feelings and would be able to feel pain. He would eventually become one of us. Barry told me that this spell should not really be used but that their arms were forced to use this magic spell.

When I heard this I started to feel really bad, how could I allow a clone of myself to take on something so evil? I knew that if he was hurt I would be hurting also. I had no choice but to stop this from happening. I ran over to my Mum and Dad but knew that there was no way of stopping the spell. The spell had created a magical barrier around the area and uses this to protect itself. This was out of my control but I had to come up with something to stop this from happening. How could I let him walk through the door and face the other side. It had to be me. I began to think if I could trick everyone into thinking that the clone had gone through the door but it was really me. There was no more I could do tonight but I needed to work through my plan. I decided to head into my room and get some sleep and cook up my plan. This had to work, I would not allow anything or anyone else to sacrifice themselves for me.

As I made my way upstairs to go to bed, I took a last look around to my parents and could still see they were in their trance like state concentrating on creating my clone. The clone was looking so scary and an exact replica of me, I needed to sort this out once and for all. I walked into my room, thinking how I could make this right. I had lots of questions running through my head about the clone, what if it had the same thoughts as me and would talk like me? I needed to shut down my brain so I would be able to get some sleep. As I slowly drifted off to sleep I could hear my Mum and Dad still casting away.

I knew morning had come as the sun slowly crept through my window and a stray ray of light was dancing across my face. I must have forgotten to close the curtains last night. I couldn't wait to get downstairs and see what had become of my clone. I jumped out of bed still in the same clothes as last night. I skidded down the hall thanks to the socks I was wearing. I run down the stairs and into the front room, there was no one around and even the green bucket and my clone had disappeared. I walked into the kitchen and my parents were nowhere to be found, I guessed they were resting after the night they had had. Suddenly someone turned around the corner into the kitchen and I could not believe what I was looking at, it was like looking in a mirror. All his facial features perfectly replicated mine and then he spoke out in a voice that was identical to mine.

'Hi I'm Joe, it's really nice to meet you. You must be Joe my brother!'

He thought I was his brother and I didn't know what else to say but to introduce myself. The other Joe went on to explain that Mum had told him that he had a brother and that we were separated at birth and we haven't seen each other since then. He was so excited to have found all of us now and thought it was so cool that he had a family that he didn't know he had. This was so very weird and I knew this was a spell as I had seen Mum, Dad and Uncle Barry create him and now here he was looking perfectly real, this threw my mind all over the place. He asked if I wanted to help make some breakfast for Mum and Dad and I suddenly found myself not liking this experience. I knew he was just a clone but I could not tell him this as I didn't want to hurt his feelings. I agreed to help and the other Joe asked me to scramble some eggs and he went about cooking some bacon.

I could not get over how much he was like me, but just as much I was not liking him being in my life, I would not let him take my place with walking through the door that still stood in the living room. I knew I needed to ask him some questions to see if my parents had programmed him to walk through that door. I needed to get him alone to do this but decided to get breakfast out the way first. After breakfast I would start planning with him and hoped that he would listen to me. The other Joe asked how I was getting on with the eggs and I told him that they were almost done. He explained that he wanted breakfast to be perfect for everyone as he didn't have long with us all. He said he only had today then he was leaving. My stomach sank when I realised that he had been programmed to walk through the door instead of me. No way was he walking through that door, I needed to stop him, this was my time to go through the door and I had to come up with a plan as soon as I could. Breakfast was almost done and the other Joe started to make some tea for everyone. I couldn't believe that he knew how to do everything as he was just a spell, the more I looked at him the more I couldn't get over how real he looked and how normal he was acting.

'Right, that's the breakfast done, let's go and give breakfast to Mum and Dad.'

'Joe we normally have breakfast in the kitchen, it's a rule of Uncle Barry's.'

'Not today Joe, I told Mum, Dad and Uncle Barry to stay in bed as I wanted to do something special for them all as it's my last day here. It's been great the last couple of weeks I have lived here and the places we have been.'

A couple of weeks I said to myself, you were only made yesterday and into this morning, but they must have put memories into his head. That was so cool to make him think like that, but cruel at the same time. This spell had truly worked but also it could be quite damaging to the clone. I agreed with the other Joe but told him that I didn't want him to go and that we could make him stay a little longer but to let everyone have their breakfast first. The other Joe picked up the breakfast tray full of steaming food. It smelt so good and he looked round to me and gave me a smile and said 'Thank you for being the greatest brother.'

I smiled back at him and replied 'Come on and let's get everyone their breakfast before it gets cold.'

As we were walking to give everyone breakfast I could not get over how the other Joe acts just like me, the little gestures he does that are exactly the same as me. The more I spoke and watched him it was getting more and more like having a twin brother. I asked myself how long this spell would last and it could only be a matter of time until it wore off. I started to hope it wouldn't as I liked having him around. I couldn't wait until after breakfast to spend some time with the other Joe and just hoped that Mum and Dad would allow me to. My plan in my head was getting better and better as even my parents would not know who was who. This could work in my favour, making everyone think it was the other Joe who walked through the door instead of me. As time ticked by I realised that I was going to be walking though that door. Regardless of how long I am away, I know the other Joe will keep everyone happy, I need to teach him how to play video games as I thought he would love that.

We both served breakfast to Mum, Dad and Uncle Barry, they were still sitting in their rooms. They told us that they would be down in the next hour and this would be my time to work on the other Joe. I asked the other Joe to come and sit in my room as I needed to talk to him. I really wanted him to listen carefully to me and wondered how he would take being a clone. I needed to put my plan into action as I did not have much time left.

'Joe do you mind coming here a moment please, there is something I need to tell you.'

'What is it Joe?' He replied.

'You know the door that you see, you should not go through it when the time comes. I want you to stay here, there is so much I need to show you. I don't want you to go yet, we are having so much fun don't you agree?"

'Yes Joe I love it here and I don't want to go either. This is something I have to do, I know it's right but I would love to stay longer but I can't.'

I asked him why as I needed to find out what he was thinking and why he shouldn't stay.

'It's strange Joe, I can't tell you why but I know that I have to go through to the door, it feels right. I know I have to leave, it wants me to go through it now, I'm excited but I have to wait. Although I will miss everyone but it's the right thing to do, I haven't got long left Joe, time is nearly up.'

Wow this spell has really been imprinted onto the clone, I shouldn't keep calling him a clone as he was called Joe. I started to think if I was to let him go through the door but then could I live with myself if I found out what Lady Malaga would do to him when she found out what he really was.

'I understand Joe and we will miss you, but I do think you should think about staying a little longer with us all.'

He looked up at me and then got up and walked off, where was he going and what was he up to? I started to follow him and found that he walked up to the black door and started to stare at it. At one point I though he was going to grab the red handle and walk through it. I managed to pull him from the door as I heard footsteps coming down the stairs and looked out into the hall and saw Mum walking down the stairs. The other Joe ran over to Mum and gave her the warmest welcome. She whispered something in his ear and he ran into the garden she called me over and said,

'I see that you have met the other Joe then, we need to just be calm around him, he thinks he's been here a while. We all know that he must leave soon through the door, just be yourself and don't act any differently. The spell has worked really well Joe and this will give us about a week I would say before Lady Malaga realises the other Joe is just a clone. We have done the spell so it looks like you and acts like you. Do you have any questions before he comes back inside?'

'Yes I do Mum, what will happen to him when she finds out? Will the spell just wear off and he will go?'

'No Joe, when we used the spell it was our last resort. You never use this spell without very good reason, the clone will become more and more human as time goes on.tTen days after the spell that we cast on him, you have a choice to save him with another spell. The spell we originally cast will protect him for ten days, no spell can harm him. We will have to bring him back here to do a second spell so he can become human and then you will have a brother Joe. If he does not make it back after the ten days, his spell will be broken so he will be in danger. Only you can bring him back by taking his place, but by that time you will be ready to face Lady Malaga. We have done this to protect you, so in the time she has him we can train you up to be the best you can be when Lady Malaga returns for you. This is a gamble we know, but your Dad and I know this is the best thing for all of us.'

This is so much to take in, I now have to save the clone which will be my brother, his life is in my hands. I have to do what's right, I was going to trick them and walk through the door, but the tables have turned. I now need to let him take my place to save him. I'm going to have a brother. What will people say? Will they think it's strange that I now have a brother. He will be my twin, I need to ask Mum some more questions.

'What will people say when we return and I have a brother, won't this be very strange Mum? I get what your saying and I have to save him, so I will do everything in my power to train to be the best I can.'

'This is where our magic comes into play Joe, if we cast the second spell on the other Joe it will also cast a spell on our whole lives and everyone that knows us too. The other Joe would have always been in our lives and we and others will know no difference.

This sounds promising, I will have a twin brother, something I have always wanted. In the time he has been around, I have realised this and I will protect my brother at all costs. I began to wonder if he had the same power as me and would I be able to train him up once I had been trained. I told Mum that I totally understood and asked if the other Joe would have the same magical powers as all of us.

'Joe, when the second spell has been cast he will have our blood so yes, you will have a twin brother, you will also be his mentor. This will be good for you Joe, as the years go by you two will grow close and you will have each others backs. You both will be so connected you can face anything together.'

Wow that had just sent shivers down my spine, we both would be able to take on anything. Once I have been fully trained, I will face Lady Malaga and save my brother, then train him up like me, we will be the power brothers. We can both face anything together.

Joe came back in from outside and I looked over at him and gave him a great big smile and he smiled back. I really liked the thought of this and I knew for sure that I now had a twin brother, I didn't see him as a clone anymore and I knew I had to do everything to keep him safe. I told my Mum that I would do everything I could to protect him and gave my Mum my word. Mum told me she was going to rest some more before we knew what was going to happen later on today. She explained that I would need to go along with anything he said as these were his memories. She told us to have fun and that she would see us later.

I really wanted to spend some time with Joe now, as the time we had together was going so fast. I really wanted to show him some of my computer games that I liked playing, I wondered if he knows how to play computer games or if I would have to teach him?

'Fancy a game on the computer Joe?'

He replied that he loved computer games and did I remember when we played for hours the other day and had a great laugh. He started to laugh uncontrollably as he said he was beating me all the time. We both raced to my room to see who would win this time. As we did a race I couldn't help but think about the memories that Mum and Dad must have planted into him when he was created and how scary this magic actually was.

I started to grab the computer and all of the games, it would be so nice to play this downstairs without disturbing Mum, Dad or Uncle Barry. There were so many wires and I made a mental note that I would need to remember how to plug them all back in. The other Joe sat on my bed laughing. I turned and asked him why he was laughing and he replied 'Why do all of that when we could do all of this.'

I was so confused by what he meant, then all of a sudden he raised his hand and said a spell. The computer and games were gone. Come with me the other Joe shouted. We ran downstairs and there it was all set up in the front room. How did he just do that? I was thinking there was no way, he shouldn't have been able to do that. This played on my mind for sometime while we were playing the computer, I couldn't get it out of my head I had to say something.

'Hey Joe, you know what you did earlier with the computer, you cast a spell in the bedroom, and made the computer appear downstairs. How did you do that? Do you know lots of spells?'

'Joe I don't know what you're on about, we carried it downstairs, we had trouble with it don't you remember?'

Well that wasn't it, I'm sure he cast a spell in the bedroom, I now started to question my own sanity. No he did do it I remember him doing it. We played the computer for a little while longer but I couldn't really focus on the game. I was still wondering how he did it. I wondered if Mum and Dad knew he could do this. I hadn't even been trained myself to do any magic yet, so how could he know how to do things straight away. I asked myself if I was to say anything to Mum, Dad or even Uncle Barry.

'That's right Joe I do remember, I was just being silly.'

He looked at me very strangely, the more I looked at him I could see something happening in his eye, there was a slight colour change. I looked more closely I could see a very slight red colour in his eye. I was thinking there was no way it could be red, that was the colour of evil. I got up quickly and I was sure he noticed what I had seen. He grabbed my arm and said.

'Whats wrong Joe, where are you going so quickly?'

I had to make an excuse up as something didn't feel quite right. Mum and Dad have made an evil version of me I'm sure of it without them even knowing. I gave a quick response back.

'I'm just going to the kitchen to make a drink would you like one?'

'Yes please Joe, hurry back we have a game to finish.'

In my head I needed to get to Mum quickly, I know what I saw and there was red in his eye. He had got his eye on my every move and I can't believe that I thought I was going to have a twin brother. This seemed like we now have an enemy in our house, we are not safe and I wondered if this was Lady Malaga's doing. Did she know what we had all been up too. I walked back with the drinks just hoping someone will wake up in a bit and come downstairs. I tried my best to be myself as I didn't want him noticing anything, I prayed for someone to wake up as I had a feeling that something bad was coming.

'Joe, I sense that you aren't being yourself at the minute, is there something up I feel your being very nervous around me?'

'Not at all Joe, I'm fine thank you just thinking when will everyone be up that's all.'

'Your not a very good lier Joe, why would you be lying to me?'

He knew that I was lying to him, he must of seen me looking at his red eye. I didn't know what to do, do I shout for help or do I play him like he is playing all of us. There was danger coming I knew it. Joe stood right in front of me and he leaned into my face and said 'It's because you just saw my red eye isn't it?'

Within seconds his whole face started to transform and stood right in front of me was the wicked Lady Malaga. She spoke in an evil voice and said 'You can think you can trick me do you? I see everything boy, how dare you try to trick me. I'm more powerful than all of you combined. I did have high hopes for you but now you've made me really angry.'

She lifted up off the floor in the other Joe's body, well the clone. The eyes were so red and the face had turned a grave black colour. She started to lift me off the floor also with her magical cloud and spoke to me again.

'This is what is going to happen now, as I'm sure you are aware, I cannot hurt this clone but i can use his body. I will have the best of fun with him for the ten days but trust me when the ten days are over I will carry on with my plan and you will say goodbye to this ghastly creation. The choice is yours Joe, you can trick your Mum and Dad into thinking the clone has gone through the door when it was really you or I will make you all pay. If he walks through my door, he will not return and you will not save him. You can save him now by walking through the door yourself. Make your choice boy, you haven't got long.'

She dropped me to the ground and left the other Joe's body. Joe looked at me from his place where he dropped to the floor. His face was utter devastation as he did not understand what had just happened. I had a feeling something bad was going to happen and it did. There was no way I was going to let the other Joe walk through that door now and I was going to stop him thinking he would. I didn't want any harm coming to my now brother and I would protect him with everything I had. I needed to think of a plan quickly to make sure I would be the one to walk through that door

Chapter 10

PLAN

I put my plan into action in my head but I needed this to be perfect. If is wasn't right I would lose the game. Lady Malaga was not happy at all so if I couldn't pull this off the other Joe would be in real danger. I had three plans running through my head and I just needed to choose which one I was going to go with.

My first plan would be that I would say that I needed to leave the house to get something for Uncle Barry as he wasn't feeling at all well. I would say that the other Joe needed to look after the house and Mum and Dad. While I was gone I would have to time the moment the other Joe had to walk through the door and then I would swap places with him. This had to work but if not I had another plan. I could hide the other Joe somewhere in the house and make out that I was actually the clone and say to my parents that the real Joe was upstairs in bed unwell. But what if I hide the other Joe and then he suddenly walked into the room and gave my plan away? I needed to be the one to walk through the black door as the other Joe's protection spell would only last ten days. After the ten days Lady Malaga could harm the other Joe or even worse, kill him. My third and final plan would be to tell the other Joe to hide in the house and not come out until I have found him. When he is hidden I would enter the door and then he was totally protected and I would be the one who was with Lady Malaga. I didn't know if the other Joe was programmed to walk through the door regardless of me intervening. This was the plan I was going to go with, I heard some movement and someone coming down the stairs, I walked into the hallway and saw that it was my Mum. She told me that she needed to talk to me. I knew Mum would have gotten up as it was nearly time for the other Joe to walk through the door. I had an hour to put my plan into action. I was going to be the one to walk through that door no matter what.

Mum told me that she wanted me to have some fun in the last hour with the other Joe, she told us to go out into the garden and play like kids should play. I decided that I could put my plan in action outside and my parents would be none the wiser. I told my Mum that we would and that would be an excellent idea. She said we would need to be back no later than 6pm as things needed to be put into place. I hugged my Mum and kissed her cheek goodbye.

'Come on Joe, let's go outside for a little bit. We can have a walk and I'll show you around the area if you would like.'

Joe ran towards me and was so happy to be allowed to get out, almost like he had been trapped in the house for a long time. He couldn't wait to put on his coat and shoes, he raced me to the front door and he won the race as he was so excited to get out. We both heard Mum shout for us to have some fun and that she would see us in a bit.

Both of us were standing outside and the front door slammed shut. I had the crazy idea to give the other Joe a race down the driveway and he was so excited that he started a countdown. We both ran down the drive as quick as our legs would take us, we both had the same running patterns and thought the same. As we got to the end of the drive the race was a draw, I said to the other Joe that when we get back to the house there was a special part of the game that I wanted to show him but you had to earn this special part of the game by hiding somewhere in the house. I explained that if I didn't find him within ten minutes, he would win by me showing him the secret level in the game. The other Joe's face lit up acting like this was the best thing ever. It was starting to look like I had the other Joe on my side now and my plan was going to work.

We made our way down towards the end of Uncle Barry's driveway, at the end there was a small winding road that you had to be very careful on due to not being able to see the cars coming. There was a slight bend in the road which made it impossible for the cars to see you crossing. Uncle Barry's house stood on a slight hill and the cars always accelerated up the hill which made it almost impossible to stop in time if someone was in the road. We checked the road both ways and made sure there were no cars coming, we crossed the road and made it to the other side. There were a group of trees stood proudly with their branches whistling in the wind and I could not help but think back to Sir George. The other Joe just stood and stared at the trees. Out of nowhere there was a ginormous crack through the air and a bolt of red lightening hit one of the trees. With an almighty groan the tree started to fall towards us and I shouted at the other Joe to watch out. I grabbed hold of him and we were forced back into the middle of the road. I heard the screech of tyres as a car slammed on their brakes. The smell of burning rubber filled the air as the car came to an abrupt stop and swerved to miss the tree that was now lying inches away from us, it had only just missed us and we were lucky to still be alive. What was meant to be us having a quiet nice walk in the country having some fun had led to us both nearly losing our lives either by a tree or being hit by a car. I heard the car door creak open and the driver got out of the car. I imagined that the driver was not going to be happy at all with us but she ran towards us in a state of shock and said 'You poor boys, are you ok? You look like you've seen a ghost, please stay here and calm down before either of you faint.'

The other Joe just looks at me and simultaneously we both start to laugh at each other. I asked him if we were ok and said that we had a close call with both the tree and the car, as we continued to laugh the driver of the car seems to be getting angrier and angrier. Suddenly she had an outburst and shouted at both of us 'Stop the pair of you will you, do you think it's funny what has just happened, we could have all lost our lives. I came to see if you were both ok, but you clearly think this situation is hilarious and that is not ok.'

She stormed back to her car and got back into the drivers seat. With a shake of her head and some odd muttering she slammed the door shut. As we both stood up and made it back towards Uncle Barry's drive we heard her car roar to life and she drove off down the road, the car swerved around the fallen tree. As she passed us she wound down the window and shouted to both of us that we should be ashamed of ourselves and made a rude gesture towards us through to window. We continued to laugh and she wound her window back up and sped down the country road.

After our laughter had died down we both could see the drivers point but that was the last we would ever see of her. A funny feeling suddenly come over my body and it felt like the moment you wake from a dream and you think you have fallen into your bed. I looked down at my watch and saw the time and looked over at Joe in horror. Time had gone so quickly and we had had some good fun regardless of what had happened. I said to the other Joe that we needed to get back to the house so that I could show him the secret that I was on about earlier on. He replied that he was super excited to find out the secret part of the game and that he was going to find the best hiding place in the house so I would never find him in the ten minute limit.

We started to head back and I keep going over in my head about the car that nearly crashed into us. As we walked back up the hill on our way back, I began to realise that this has been such a crazy time since I saw the bright light in the sky to what has happened to me and all of us, this is like being in a movie. I now know there was so much more to come, we reached the long driveway and the other Joe runs towards the front door, he cant wait for the surprise, but he is going to be disappointed as there isn't one. The only thing I'm doing is saving him, I hope he forgives me but there is no other way, I start to think what Mum, Dad and Uncle Barry will think, they will be so mad with me but I have no other choice I have to do what Lady Malaga says. I also ran up to the front door and the other Joe opens the door the stairs are straight opposite and the coast is clear. We both leg it up the stairs so no one can see us. I shout up to Joe who is just above me, 'Go and hide Joe but remember don't come come out until I find you, if I don't find you in ten minutes then meet me back in my room.'

He replied 'Ok Joe this is so much fun, you won't find me.'

I closed my eyes and began counting to 10. The plan was working and my next mission was to get to the door, I just hoped Mum and Dad were not watching every move I was making. I couldn't see them around and wondered if they were in the kitchen. I decided to leave it around five minutes before the black door opened up and I could run through it with out anyone stopping me. I would watch everyone's movements from the landing and my timing would be everything now. I headed towards the landing and started my stake out, I could hear my Mum, Dad and Uncle Barry in the kitchen, they were talking about it being nearly time for the door to open. I heard Dad asking where were the two Joes and Mum replied saying we were upstairs playing games. I heard Uncle Barry make his way into the front room and sit down to watch the door. There was no sign of Mum and Dad yet as they had decided not to join Uncle Barry. I thought about writing a quick letter to my parents to explain everything so i made a dash to my room to grab my note pad and pen.

Mum and Dad

Please don't be mad with me and what I decided to do, I had no choice and I didn't want to worry you both but Lady Malaga showed up and knew what was happening. She warned me that if the other Joe walked through the door and once the spell had broken after ten days she would harm him and possibly kill him. I needed to save him as I have always wanted a brother and I must walk through the door myself. I really wanted to tell you both but I didn't want any harm coming to the other Joe, when he first arrived I wasn't sure if I liked him, but I got used to him being around as my twin and it feels like he's always been here even though he was created by magic. After all this is over he will be a part of all of us. I don't even know if this letter will be erased when he becomes fully human, so you can see why I have done what I have done. I love you both very much, say hello to Uncle Barry for me and I love him too. Once Lady Malaga has finished with me I would have been trained by her too, even though you both didn't want it this way. I will come back fully trained and we all can beat Lady Malaga once and for all. Please take care of yourselves, I don't know how long I'll be gone but i'm leaving you as a boy and I will return as a man. Please treat Joe as you would if it was me and in the way you would if I hadn't really gone. Lots of love,

Joe (Your real son).

I leave the note on my bed, and looked down at my watch and saw that it was nearly time to face my destiny. There was only fifteen minutes until the door opened. Some part of me was quite excited and another part was scared but when I think about it Lady Malaga was kind at some point, you never know she might be completely different with me on my own. She was going to train me and I was going to learn to be one of the most powerful magic wielders in the world. Well my magic lessons start soon and she will help me and I can then face her when I am trained and ready.

I thought she would act all nasty at first and then soften down, she must have a warm heart somewhere. I head towards the landing and Uncle Barry was still there watching the door, Mum walked in with Dad and they both sat down. I walked downstairs almost silently and watched from the edge of the room for the door to open then I could make a run for it. Just before the door was due to open, I heard footsteps on the stairs and quickly looked back to see who it was and I could see the other Joe walking towards me. He shouted out 'Joe, what are you doing?'

My cover was blown and I had no other choice but to make a run for it, I heard both my parents shout at me to stop but I had just one thing on my mind. I ran to the door like my life depended on it and I could feel the adrenaline flow through my body.

Everything suddenly went fuzzy and I couldn't see anyone in the front room any more, I heard the creak of a door and could see the black door opening right in front of me. I continued to run towards the door and all I could hear where the echos of people calling my name. When I was within reaching distance of the door, I started to slide the rest of the way and could feel myself begin to fall into a pitch black dark hole. I realised that I had made it into the door and my plan was a success after all. I was about to find out if I had made either the best or worst decision in my life.

Chapter 11

THE DARK WORLD

I continued to fall through the darkness and through the whistling wind I could hear a cackling laugh travelling towards me getting louder and louder. I wondered where I was falling and then the laugh became unbearable as it pierced through the dark and started assaulting my eardrums. The sound got louder and louder and then I heard her. Lady Malaga was the one laughing and her laughter suddenly died down and she said 'Welcome my child, welcome.' I continued to fall for what felt like for an eternity and then suddenly hundreds upon hundreds of faces filled the air and she spoke again.

'Don't be sacred child, you are not falling to your death, that would be too easy, you are entering my world now. I hope you enjoy the fall from your world into mine, you belong to me now and you will do what I demand of you. You and I have a lot to do, you are nearly with me and I am a vision from your imagination. A word of warning to you, mind the drop.' With that the vision ended and the laughter and faces disappeared.

Drop, what drop was she on about? I was already falling, suddenly a clear hole started to form as I continued to fall. Through it I could see a river and I dropped into the centre of it. The ripples and current through the river were so strong and nearly knocked me below the surface a few times. I could see a bank on the other side and knew I had to make it. Just a few more strokes I kept telling myself as I battled against the current and riptide. I reached the bank and dragged myself up and collapsed onto my back to get my breath, that was harder than I ever thought possible. I scrambled to my feet and could make out a cottage on the edge of the horizon. I walked towards it and soon the cottage was right in front of me. Dotted around the cottage were hundreds of trees, these trees were nothing like the ones at home, they looked almost dead with their leaves decorating the floor beneath them. Down through the trunks stood black fissures, this made the trees look like they had been the victims of magic. As I continued to walk towards the cottage the evil cackling laugh from earlier on filled the air, at the sound of the laughter the trees all opened their eyes and they were a dirty shade of red. They started to advance towards me. As quick as the laughter had started it again stopped and a voice that sent chills through my body spoke out to me. 'You think you're strong enough do you? Well here lies your first test, show me what you've got, oh and have this to help you out.'

A magic light started to swirl around my hands and a sword started to materialise within my clasped hand.

It was decorated an odd black colour and I could barely hold it up due to the weight of the steel, that made up the blade. The trees continued their advance towards me and I knew this was my chance to show her what I was made of. The tree nearest to me swiped its branch towards me and I dodged out of the way just in time. I had had enough of trees attacking me, so I summoned all the strength I had and brought the sword above my head, and with a sickening thud, I swung the sword. This hit the tree's branch dead through the middle and the sword moved through its branch like a knife through butter. I kept doing this time and time again with the remaining trees, as I continued my assault on the trees the sword began to glow an odd shade of blue and suddenly a lightening bolt pierced through the air and hit the remaining trees. The figure that was standing outside the cottage moved towards me and lowered their hood, it was Lady Malaga and she wore a shocked but impressed look upon her face. She spoke softly out to me that was barely a whisper and she seemed to choke out the words of kindness that she spoke, 'Well done child, you have it in you after all, don't you?'

She rose her hand and cast a spell and the trees all appeared back in their original places, no longer wielding their branches and weapons and their eyes firmly shut. She called out for me to follow her, she walked slowly inside the cottage and left the door open for me to follow. As I walked I was terrified the trees would come back to life as I did not have enough energy to battle them yet again. I kept hold of the sword the entire way but as I reached the door, the swords spell vanished along with the sword itself. I looked into the cottage and could see her sitting beside the fire, she turned her head towards me and said,

'Come on in child, I won't hurt you, I am so impressed with what you have just done. You and I have a lot to do, you will give me what I want from you, and in return I will train you to be the best you can be. At the end of your training, you will remember the spell that I want. After that we go our separate ways, but if you try to stop me I will destroy you.'

She laughed out loud with the wicked laugh that she had, I realised that this was my time to be powerful and she didn't seem all that bad really maybe we could be friends after all.

'Now you will listen to me at all times, you will have your own room where you can practice magic and learn from all my spell books. I will not have you messing me around, do I make myself clear? The only time we will talk is when I train you personally then you will go back to your room. I have rules and if you break these the freedom you have now will be no longer, you will become my prisoner.'

Ok, I thought we could be friends but this isn't good I'll have to do what she says. I went to sit down and she cast a spell to transport me to my room that she had mentioned earlier. It was a good sized room and the walls were made from exposed brick, the door was sealed shut with what I presumed was magic and the view from the window looked out onto a path that was flanked either side by the same trees that I had recently faced. I looked around and spotted a bed in one corner of the room and I must admit, it looked incredibly comfortable right now. The walls were lined with shelf upon shelf filled with dusty books that contained centuries of magical learning. I walked over the the desk and sat proudly against the wall was a letter addressed to me. I hastily tore open the letter and read its contents.

Rules and regulations between apprentice and master

This is a magical binding contract between the two parties involved, if at any time the rules listed below are broken or if you fail to comply with any instruction, you will be stripped of your magic and sent back to the world from which you come or become my prisoner. This contact must be signed by both parties using a single drop of their own blood. Find all rules that you must comply with below, once signed this contract cannot be broken unless any rule is broken and then this contract would be destroyed.

Rules:

1. No harm will come to to you whilst you are training

2. You have the freedom to practice outside

3. No rules are to be broken

4. No freedom will be allowed upon failure of any magical tests

5. You must show the upmost respect to everyone whilst you are here.

There was a space below for the drop of blood that was deemed necessary to make the contract magically binding. It looked like I might be at this place for a while whilst I trained, I thought back to Mum and Dad and wished they could have been the ones to train me, but I had to make this decision, I was given no other choice. I went over to the door and attempted to pull it open but it would not budge, I was trapped in here, I wanted to get out and explore my new residence. I looked around the room and noticed a board had appeared on the wall, this was not here earlier. I read the instructions on the notice board and it explained that whilst I was here, I would have to stick to a routine and my training schedule would follow shortly. Suddenly a knock on the door scared the life of out me and someone behind the door spoke out and said '

Welcome to Lady Malaga's headquarters, I will be your personal magical guide whilst you stay with us. I will shortly be giving you a tour of the grounds and of course the training area. If you need any help whilst you are here, you must come to me, your door is timed and will only open at certain points of the day. Please get ready as your door will open in ten minutes, I will be back shortly.'

This was crazy, I now had my own magical guide and I began to wonder what he looked like and what his name was. I followed the instruction to get myself ready and began to feel a slight feeling of homesickness, but realised the quicker I got the training complete the quicker I could get back to my family. Suddenly the door opened and there stood my magical guide smiling back at me. He spoke in an animated voice and said,

'Hello Joe, my name is Blue, it's very nice to meet you. Please don't be scared of me, I used to be human but the witch turned me into this. I will be your magic guide if you need anything I'll be happy to help. As you noticed there is a notice board and we have a very strict routine here Joe, you are only allowed out once the door is opened. It isn't too bad Joe you will get used to our way of life. You will be out of your room for your breakfast, lunch, dinner and training, this will be provided by myself and others like me, who you will meet shortly. Joe you will be here as long as it takes you to pass all of your training then once you have passed right at the end you will have to see Lady Malaga, she is the only one that can release you. This sounds like a lot to take in Joe but please don't feel sad, be happy you won't see Lady Malaga at all, so we do try our best to make this place as happy and fun as we can.'

Blue was really cute and he was not human, he was all blue and short with red eyes. He almost looked like an elf and elves were known to be friendly. This didn't sound as bad as I thought and I had really thought I would have been training with Lady Malaga. I was getting so excited and thought about getting this show on the road.

'So Joe, there will be times where we all have to gather for Lady Malaga's announcements, these will be held in the large gardens which I will show you shortly, don't worry you aren't the only one with the door on a timer, we all are. We are slaves to Lady Malaga and we all have jobs to do. Right let's get going I'm going to show you the gardens and where you will be training. You will meet some of my friends along the way, also there are others here just like you, there are rules to follow when we enter the gardens which you must follow and never break.' Blue explained.

This felt somewhat like a holiday but a part inside me knew deep down that I was being held prisoner here in Lady Malaga's headquarters. Blue walked me out of my room and down a long walkway, where there were big archways covering the path. This lead to an open space where there are so many beautiful trees and flowers. Right in the middle was a big square patch and this is where I would be sitting my magical tests Blue told me. Further along were stunning walkways and running alongside them were streams decorated with bridges this was like something out of a book, It was truly amazing. On the far side of the horizon Blue pointed out a place which was forbidden due to there being so much darkness and danger. This was known as the dark gardens and if you ventured there, you would not return, only Lady Malaga was known to enter this place and return safely. That was a place I wouldn't want to go as it sounded so dark and scary. Blue pointed out a beautiful fountain which had water cascading down its facade. I looked closely and noticed that the water was tinged with pink and had hints of gold glitter running through it. It was beautiful and not only was the colour lovely but I was told it also had its own healing power, we are allowed to enter the fountain if we are ever hurt through training. This is only offered to us while we are training, once you pass the training you are not allowed to enter it. If you attempted to, it would harm you. There is a curse on the water, which allows healing and gives you protection from Lady Malaga whilst training only. Blue goes on to tell me we are allowed to meet up with other apprentices that are also learning magic, but warns me not to get to close to anyone as they are being trained to work for Lady Malaga. I'm only here for two reasons, to learn the magic and to remember the spell that I created years and years ago. I really wanted to get to know more about Blue, what was he like before he turned into Blue, what was his real name and did he have a family? I found myself thinking about what this place was like before Lady Malaga took it over. I headed over to the water fountain as the water was beckoning me over to it. Through the trickling water I saw someone looking at me, she had long green hair and her body was also green, the only thing that was not green was her red eyes. Blue spoke out, 'Joe please meet Mrs Green, Mrs Green is one of my close friends and she also has been changed. Mrs Green provides all the food and helps me with some of the magical tests, she doesn't like lazy people and you must always be willing to help. If you don't she can get very angry, Mrs Green is very powerful and you will learn a lot from her.'

I walked around to meet Mrs Green and she just stood there with her arms crossed looking very angry. Mrs Green's hair was blowing in the wind and I noticed tiny silver spikes running through her hair, they were shining in the hot sun and I thought that I had better introduce myself. 'Hello Mrs Green I'm Joe, it's very nice to meet you. I love your hair the glint of it is catching my eye, I'm really looking forward to learning magic with you.'

'Welcome Joe, I will also be training you, I must warn you that I don't like lazy people at all. I won't hear any excuses lad as I am not here to waste my time, I will show you everything once and that is it, do be careful of my hair, it tends to have a mind of it's own, the spikes can lash out every now and then. If I become angry, the spikes will be released, they have only injured a few people but the water can heal you. I can't control them, only my temper can, it was a curse put on me by Lady Malaga, so you must do your best not to make me angry.'

It sounded awful that Mrs Green had been cursed and that her long hair no longer had a mind of its own. I knew I could not and would not make her angry or at least try my best. I told Mrs Green that I would not want to upset her and thank you for the warning. Mrs Green nodded her head in approval, her arms were still crossed and blue beckoned me back over to him. He explained that Mrs Green was his very good friend and that they both would be helping me through my magical tests. He also told me that he wanted to introduce me to another one of his friends, who was called Mr Fire. I followed blue through the grounds and walked past lots of flower beds with all manner of plants climbing towards the sun. The smells that were coming from some of the bushes reminded me of the sweet shops I would visit with my Mum back in my world. We came across an unusual mound of flowers piled on top of each other and from inside came a strange buzzing sound. I could also hear someone rustling behind the mound of flowers. Blue shouted out, 'There you are Mr Fire, please meet our new apprentice Joe.'

I saw a head poke its way through the mound of flowers and knew that this was Mr Fire. His whole body was red and looked really scary, a hand shot through the flowers and grabbed hold of mine, he shouted out loudly, 'What do we have here then, do you think you are worthy of learning the art of magic? I want to see what you have got, show me some magic, I don't like unwanted magical people who possess no abilities. I must warn you that if you show me something useless I will have no option but to set my bees on you.'

Blue warns me that Mr Fire is very set in his own ways and doesn't like people not taking things seriously. He does have the power to set his bees on people to keep them in line. The sting of the bees are like burns from fire and this isn't against any of the rules as the water will heal you. This is to make sure you take everything he was teaching to you in and to make sure you know it isn't a game. Blue told me that a lot of the time Mr Fire sets his bees on his students to make them work harder. If they aren't working hard the bees will hover over them and give them thirty minutes to get their magic up to scratch and if not they will feel a sting from the bee.

'Hello Mr Fire, it's very nice to meet you, I love what you are doing with the flowers that must have taken you ages to do. What lovely weather there is and it's great to be out here with the flowers, really good to meet you.'

Blue stared at me and shook his head at me and I whispered to Blue, 'had I taken my greeting too far?' Mr Fire shouted at me,

'You think you're funny do you? Do you want me to set a bee on to you? If I do you won't find yourself funny. I suggest you leave me, now go.'

I realised that I had taken it too far and I needed to get away from Mr Fire as I did not fancy being stung by his bees. Blue pulled me away as he wanted to show me where we were to eat all the meals. I waved goodbye to Mr Fire and he scowled at me. The grounds of the headquarters was huge, and there was so much to feast my eyes on. In the distance I could see rows and rows of huge mushrooms. I turned to Blue and asked what they were used for and Blue replied they are used for when the apprentices practice magic. They are enchanted to become your enemy whilst you practice, don't be fooled they are quick and nasty when they attack. You will see them in action from tomorrow, today is the tour of your new home and our way of life. We walked past the rows and rows of the mushrooms and came in to a building. The building had no doors or windows, as we walked inside I could see a large wooden table situated in the centre of the building. Where the stools would be were just stumps of old manky wood. Towards the back of the building you could see the open plan kitchen, this looked very basic and not very comfortable at all. Blue spoke out to me when he saw the horror on my face. 'Joe this is where you come for all your meals, it's not the best of rooms in the headquarters and was not designed for comfort. Lady Malaga demands no one be in here for any longer than thirty minutes. Your ring on the finger has a time spell on it and if you;re in here longer than thirty minutes an alert will be sent to her.'

'What will happen if she finds out blue?'

'Put it this way, someone was chained in a chamber for days and the rumours have it that they weren't fed or given any water but we don't know the full details Joe. I don't want to find out either, I pray everyday we can find a way to break free from Lady Malaga, but we just haven't got the power and strength. Anyway that's enough from me, shall we move on?'

That didn't sound good at all and I wouldn't want to be in the hall for any longer than I needed. I wondered if i could get my food and take it to eat outside or even in my room but I guessed that would also be a no. I asked Blue another question about his life before Lady Malaga took over but Blue said we have to hurry back to our rooms before the doors magically sealed again. As we hurried back to our rooms Blue explained to me that I was the first person to ask such a question as others just came to learn magic and that was all. He also explained that Lady Malaga only wanted the best ones to come through headquarters, if they didn't make it they were cast to the ends of the world. He explained that we don't tend to ask questions about what happened to the ones who had vanished. He apologised and said that he had gone off topic and would answer my original question.

'Well this place was where we lived and worked for many many years, we would have guests arrive and stay for many weeks at a time. This was a place where you could just come and relax, there would be shows put on with evening banquets laden with the best food. Since Lady Malaga arrived she took over and turned us into her slaves, the building where we have our meals used to be the most beautiful hall you have ever seen. Lady Malaga destroyed everything, the dark garden is where she would perform her magic and the more magic she performed the darker the garden became. So you see Joe, she has changed all our lives, we work for her now. There were some people that refused and she killed them right on the spot with her evil magic. We would give anything to be set free but we are all friends and some of us are even family. We need to hurry Joe, our time outside is nearly up.'

I had finally found what the history of this place actually was and I made it my aim to come back here and set everyone free from this hell they were living in. Lady Malaga cannot get away with this, I knew I was currently her slave but I would bide my time and when I was strong enough I would come back and free this land of her once and for all. As I walked to my room, I could see doors all along the corridor, these belonged to other apprentices and I would need to make some friends whilst I was here. I needed to make this the best experience I could whilst I was here, as I approached my room, the door swung open and Blue turned to look at me and said, 'Well here you go Joe, back to your room, you will be able to see that your notice board will have changed and will continue to do so when your magical tests are scheduled for you. This will become your diary as such and you will need to get to know your routine.'

I thanked Blue and walked into my room, just as I turned to say goodbye to him, the door slammed shut and sealed itself to prevent me from leaving. I looked up to the notice board and saw it change before my very eyes.

8am - 9am Breakfast

10am - 1pm Training

1pm - 2pm Lunch

2pm - 4pm Training

4pm - 6pm Rest (In your room)

6pm - 7pm Dinner

7pm - 8am Rest (In your room)

That didn't sound too bad really, I heard Blue shout through the door that I should use this time to read the books that adorned my walls. I was warned to only practice actual magic outside as there was a rule against magic within our rooms. All I wanted to do was relax on my bed before I had to go to dinner. I lay down on my bed and started to think about my family at home and wondered how the other Joe was getting on. How would anyone know the difference between us and he could even take my place at school. I couldn't even call my family to see how they were. She could not and will not get away with this.

Chapter 12

LADY MALAGA'S HEADQUARTERS

As the time passed whilst I was thinking about my family, my door swung open and I knew it was time for dinner. Blue said he would meet me outside my room and this would be the first time I would be eating a meal here and also meeting everybody else. I got up from my bed, he was waiting for me outside and we started the walk down to the meal hall. As we entered the hall I could hear the hum of everyone else inside. I looked around and there where hundreds of people around and I suddenly felt nervous as I hadn't met anyone yet. Blue turned to me and said 'Joe, please don't speak to the people who have red jumpers on, they are Lady Malaga's personal army and they will attack you without thinking. They are above the rules set to you. We keep away from them but anyone wearing a blue jumper is safe to meet and talk to. Come on let's eat, we need our strength.'

I looked around and could see a sea of red jumpers but they looked like everyone else, nothing different about them at all. I would listen to Blue and stay away though, I joined the line to get my food but I could not see any menu to see what we would be eating. I was behind a girl in line and could see she had the longest blonde hair, the evening light shone onto the hair and it sparkled beautifully. Someone pushed behind me and I fell into the girl in front and she turned and said 'Do you mind, you just pushed right into me, what do you think you are doing?'

I didn't know where to look as I was totally embarrassed, I apologised to the girl who I was pushed into, she then tutted and turned back around. I could not believe my luck when I was pushed again but this time I did not just knock into the girl in front, I slammed into her, she whipped around to face me again and shouted at me 'I don't know who you think you are Mr, but don't think you can just push me and get away with it. I want a word with you outside now.'

She turned and headed outside and I thought could this get any worse on my first night. I walked out after her and tried to explain but she was having none of it. I tried to explain that it was one of the red jumper lads causing all the trouble. I thought she was going to be really angry but to my surprise she was all smiles and happy and introduced herself to me and said she was glad she had an excuse to come outside as she hated the food that was served. She told me her name was Lara and that it was really nice to meet me. We stayed outside and chatted for a little bit and before we knew it, our time was up and we decided to meet up tomorrow. She said she wanted to tell me about the people that i would get to know and those to stay away from. It was so nice to be able to talk to someone who was my own age, we didn't have much time to get back to our rooms. We decided to go back to the hall and grab a quick snack. All that was left was dried up bread which was coated with a spread that smelt like chicken. Lara was right about the food here and told me she had sometimes resorted to creating her own food from magic, she promised to show me this tomorrow after my training. I met back up with Blue on my way back to my room and he explained that Lara was a lovely person but she had been caught on several occasions using magic outside of our allotted lessons and tests. I didn't admit to him that Lara wanted to show me some magic to be able to create our own food, this would be our secret. I thanked Blue for this evening and for showing me around earlier on and that I would see him tomorrow morning. As i walked into my room, the door slammed shut and sealed itself until tomorrow morning when it would reopen. I could not get what Lara had told me out of my head and thought this was totally incredible, I wanted to see if I could find this spell in the books that covered the wall. I picked up the heaviest and dustiest book off the shelf and blew on the front cover. It was a book called 'Know the magic within.' This book seemed a good place to start, I flicked through the book to see if I could see the spell that Lara was on about, but I did not find it at all. This book was all about channelling your magic but nothing to help with getting some food. I thought she must have got the spell from somewhere within her room and began to wonder if all the apprentices had the same books, I looked over at the notice board and saw that it had changed yet again. It was not showing me the spells I would be learning tomorrow, each spell appears once the previous one was fully written on the notice board.

Learn how to use your ring to cast magic

Learn how to protect yourself

Learn to control your enemies

Disarm your enemies

I read the board and my eyes lit up, I could not believe this was finally happening and I would be learning the same magic that my Mum and Dad hold. I knew that it would be dangerous to learn but once I had completed all my tests I would be ready to show everyone what I had become. I began to think about the other Joe and how much fun we had had with each other in such a short amount of time. I walked to my window and just started to stare. Lara popped up in my thoughts and I thought how nice she seemed and that I hoped that I would be training with her. Suddenly something flew past my window and dive bombed towards the ground. I saw it land on its legs and start to bury itself. It all happened so fast and I made a mental note to find out tomorrow what it was. I wanted to get out there now but I knew I was locked in for the night. I thought back to the day I had just had and thought how crazy all this was, but I knew I needed some sleep ready for the days lessons tomorrow. I collapsed onto my bed and before I knew it I had fallen asleep due to pure exhaustion.

The next morning came and as usual Blue was waiting for me outside my room. He said that today was the big day as I was finally going to be using magic and that Mrs Green would be there too. My heart jumped at the mention of her name as she seemed nice yesterday but I didn't want to make her angry as I didn't fancy being attacked by her spikes. Blue also mentioned that Mr Fire might pop over as well and after the start I had with him yesterday i was not looking forward to the experience of being stung by his bees. We joined the line for breakfast and all that was served was runny porridge that was cold and tasteless. I hastily ate my breakfast to mask the non existent taste.

I made my way over to the training ground and so many others had gathered, I turned to look at everyone but they all kept themselves to themselves. Blue started my first lesson and called me over to him, he muttered a spell to wake up his ring, he made it look so easy and said that it was now my turn. He explained that I would have to say the spell like I meant it otherwise the ring would not wake up or work. I thought this would be easy but this was not the case. I said the spell that Blue did just moments before but nothing happened. I could feel the stares from Mrs Green and Mr Fire and she shouted out that I was not ready and that I had not cleared my mind. I could sense that Mrs Green was getting angry and could feel the wind had started to pick up. Mrs Green pushed back her hair and as she did I noticed the silver spikes and remembered what I was told yesterday. Suddenly four spikes came hurtling towards me from her hair and shot into my leg. The force of the blow made me fall to my knees and I cried out in pain. Blue looked horrified as he didn't think Mrs Green would do this on my first attempt at magic. She started to laugh and so did Mr Fire, the only one to show any resemblance of care was Blue. He told me to hurry over to the fountain where I would be healed, I hobbled over to the fountain and swung my legs over the edge and into the trickling water, suddenly the spikes vanished and the pain was wiped away, it was like I had never been injured at all. I spun back around and could see Lara making her way over to me, she told me that this had happened the very first time she had practiced with Mrs Green, she also explained that over time I would get to know Mrs Green and when she was going to attack. I thought that she was being so very strict and almost bordered on being cruel but i remembered that this was not her fault but the curse that had been placed upon her by Lady Malaga. Lara said she had only popped over to

173

see if I was ok and that she was learning something called the ghost spell. She said it was really exciting and she would tell me all about it at dinner later.

I headed back over to Blue and he told me not to worry as not everyone got it on their first go and some never managed to get it at all and then Lady Malaga cast them to the ends of the world. He told me that if he was ever set free, he would make it his mission to find the cast out apprentices and save them all. We get back to the training and finally after three attempts I achieved the spell. I now needed to keep practicing so that I would be able to do the spell with no problems. I saw Lara claps her hands and mouths well done over to me. I waved back to say thank you. Mr Red saw everything and walked over towards me and said 'Can you keep your attention on class please, no speaking with others thank you.'

I said that I was sorry but I was super excited to have learnt my first spell. He wasn't at all happy with me I could feel it from him but I didn't really understand why. Blue showed me the second spell to learn and this was a protection spell, he cast the spell and he was surrounded by a magical bubble all around him, he told to me pick up a rock that lay strewn on the floor and throw it at him. I picked up the rock and it was that big and heavy I could barely throw it but I managed to and all it did was bounce off Blue. The spell was so impressive as he stopped the protection bubble around him he told me that it was my turn. He issued a word of warning that if I didn't complete the spell correctly there would be a painful aspect of failing. Apparently my hands would fill with tiny blood blisters and each time. I got it wrong some would burst and that some students take around twenty times to master the spell. He told me I would not be able to go to heal my hands until the test was complete. I asked why we would feel pain each time we conjured a spell and he told me that this was the magic's way of seeing if we were worthy of such a gift. I attempted the spell and again nothing happens, my hands start to fill with the nasty blood filled blisters. The pain from them was excruciating. Blue calls time on the class and says it's time for lunch. I can't believe that I am going to be made to go to lunch like this as it was made clear I would not be able to use the fountain until I had mastered the spell.

 Blue and I walk to get our lunch and I can see Blue looking at me, as I hold in the pain covering up my hand with my jumper sleeve. He says to me that he knows I can do this and that I have to be strong and don't give up. We walk through the building and I'm trying not to show I'm in any pain and draw any intention to myself, the place was filled with all the other apprentices. I could see Lara sitting eating her lunch, she called me over to sit with her. I queued up in line waiting for my lunch which was chicken soup and bread, I really liked soup so today I looked forward to my lunch. I grabbed a bowl of soup and started to walk over to Lara, all of a sudden one of my blisters popped, pain shot through my hand and caused me to drop the bowl of soup. It smashed down on the floor sending shards of broken crockery and soup everywhere. I yelled out as the pain intensified, everyone looked around at me and started to snigger. I could hear whispers across the hall with people saying things like idiot and that I couldn't pass the simple protection spell test.

All those who were wearing red jumpers gathered around me and started to push and pull at me whilst laughing. I thought I was done for as there was so many of them, one of the boys pulled me up from the floor and said 'We haven't seen you around here before newbie, we all know what happens to newbies who cant pass the simple protection test.' The group started to laugh yet again and I started to think that this was like any other place with it's bullies. Suddenly, whilst all the other reds continued to taunt and laugh at me, my finger started to light up and my ring cast out a spell which passed through me and all those standing around me. I see Blue run towards me and congratulate me on successfully casting the protection spell. I didn't understand how I cast the spell as I had never muttered any words and Blue explained that I must have been thinking of the spell for my ring to react to my minds thoughts.

I was so happy that I had managed to cast my second spell but the looks of the reds faces told me a different story, I even heard one of them shout out that I was to watch my back. At this point I didn't really care as I was elated to have been successful without even trying. Lara stands up and starts to clap and I look over to her and smiled in the way of a thank you. Blue comes back and sits down and hands me a fresh bowl of soup and tells me to eat up. I eat about half of the bowl and then tell Blue I can't eat anymore as my hand is so painful. I beg for him to allow me to use the fountain to heal my hand and he gives his permission. I dash out of the hall and into the gardens, the fountain is calling to me and I make my way over and throw my hand under the healing waters. As soon as the water touches my hand, the pain immediately evaporates and the blisters start to subside as if they were never meant to be there.

Suddenly the ground starts to shake and people start running from the hall and form up around the training grounds, I can hear some of them saying that she's coming and to hurry up and get into position. In the centre of the training ground, black smoke starts to unfurl and the air was filled with a dreadful cackle of laughter and I knew this was Lady Malaga. From within the smoke she starts to appear and looks over each and every one of us, after her inspection she speaks in a voice that was dripping with sarcasm and sounds so horribly evil, 'Hello my apprentices, it has come to my attention that some of you just haven't got what it takes to become a part of my army, you were warned about this and I haven't got time for time wasters.'

Her finger traces through the crowds until it lands on a particular boy I had noticed training in Lara's class, a red shot of light jumps from her finger and hits the boy square in the chest. He started to lift off the floor and as he did a cage made from rotten steel started to form around the boy. Lady Malaga looked over her handy work and started to laugh. She shouts at him 'You're wasting my time and resources here boy, I have no use for time wasters.'

I can hear him beg to be given another chance and that he was sorry but no matter what he said, it was falling upon deaf ears. Another shot of red light and I just knew he had been cast to the ends of the world. She looks over us all again and issues a warning, she said that she was watching each and everyone of us including the staff and if any of us dared to disappoint then she would not hesitate to send us to the ends of the world also. At this the smoke disappeared and so did she. Everyone was in shock and there was a flurry of movement as everyone got back into training mode to avoid being a disappointment. Blue comes over to me and says that we should not mess with Lady Malaga as she was just too strong and powerful. I knew for certain that I needed to help everyone here and all those that had been banished.

Blue attempted to carry on with the afternoon's training but I could tell he was shaken to the core with what had happened earlier. He explained that it wasn't a nice experience and hated it when it happened. He kept on asking me to do the spell I had already learnt and by the time he next came up to me I was nearly a pro at that spell. He watched my next attempt and I could see how impressed he was by his facial features. He told me that he could see something different in me to the other students and that he wanted to show me a more complex spell. He told me he was going to show me the caging spell, he explained this would come in handy with the bullies that were the reds and that he knew they would attempt to come after me because of what had happened at lunch. He told me that I shouldn't really be using this spell as this was for people that were far more advanced in their magical training than I was. He explained that we had been separated into groups depending on the path that had been chosen for us by Lady Malaga and the backgrounds we had come from. I explained that I had already been told that the yellows were good natured people and that the reds would be bad, and he confirmed that this was correct. He said that we were all called warlocks and that there were indeed two types of us. Blue told me that all yellow warlocks whilst at the headquarters could be turned into red warlocks against their will to fight for Lady Malaga. She would use the control spell on all she decided that she needed to fight, this was only a temporary spell as she had never found the ultimate spell of control. I kept it to myself that I could have been the key to this spell as I knew that if Blue found out he would treat me a whole lot differently. She was not going to get this spell from me because if she did the whole world would be doomed. I suddenly remembered that the spell I had created in my past life was to bring things back from the dead and not to control people, but I had only been told of one spell I had created previously. What if I had created the ultimate control spell also.

Blue speaks directly to me and tells me that I need to watch everything very closely as there could be some really bad side effects if this spell goes wrong but that he believed in my ability. Blue starts to cast and I watch intently not wanting to miss anything. In the distance I can see Mr Fire and his meddling nose running towards us. He shouts over to Blue and says 'What do you think you are doing, showing him that spell.'

Blue stops the spell and shouts back at Mr Fire, 'Keep your voice down will do, I don't want the whole training class to know, I have to do this for his sake and protection, so mind your own business.'

Mr Fire said he would go along with Blue on one condition, that he would set his bees hovering around me whilst I complete this spell. He added in a twist and explained that the bees would start to sting in ten minutes instead of the usual thirty minutes and that I would have just the one attempt, at first Blue was hesitant to go along with the plan but explained to me, that regardless of Mr Fire I needed to learn this spell to keep me safe from the reds. He said that as soon as I knew this spell the reds would leave me alone and even attempt to be my friend and that was a path I must choose to go down.

Blue starts to show me the spell again but this time Mr Fire has his bees ready to be let loose on me. I focussed intently on Blue and how he was casting the spell and you would have thought this was easy, just saying a few words and the spell was cast. This wasn't the case you had to prove your worth to your ring, it was the ring that decided if you were worthy of the magic it held. If you failed on the first attempt then you could attempt it again a few days later and if not then, well we all knew what happened then. The more spells you learnt the more stones your ring acquired and the more powerful you become, that's why the reds were more powerful as they had more stones than any other apprentice. The only other people more powerful than the reds were Lady Malaga's staff and of course Lady Malaga herself.

I started to cast out and Mr Fire set his bees hovering above my head, I tried my best not to let myself become distracted by this. I began muttering the spell that Blue had taught me and nothing happened, suddenly a sharp pain stabbed through my neck, the pain was the worst pain I had felt to date and I dropped to the floor, I hear Blue shout for me to get up but as I attempted to another stabbing pain hit the side of my chest and I fell to the floor once again. Whilst I lay there trying to compose myself another stabbing pain hit me in the leg and that was me done for, I closed my eyes and passed out. I felt someone pick me up from the floor and groggily opened my eyes and saw that it was Blue and Mr Fire, they were carrying me over to the fountain to be healed. I heard Blue say to Mr Fire that he should not have shown me the spell and that Mr Fire was right about not being ready. He started to shout at Mr Fire for his use of damn right cruel methods of teaching. I felt the pain instantly leave my body the minute the water touched me and I come round instantly. I look at Blue and he looks so sorry for me and says 'I'm really sorry to have put you through that Joe, Mr Fire was right in saying that you were not ready, you'll get there though and you'll be fine now.'

I lifted myself out of the water and it never ceased to amaze me at how great I felt after coming from the fountain. I suddenly remembered what I had seen the night before from my bedroom window. Blue calls out to me and says that it's time to return to my room. Without thinking I ran off and waved goodbye to Blue. I raced to the outside of my window and knelt down and started to sift through the earth where I saw the flying object bury itself last night. Suddenly my fingers scraped across something that was silver, I kept digging around it but knew that it had to be fairly deep into the ground. I knew I had minutes before my door was sealed shut and made the rash decision to cover up the hole I had dug with the twigs and leaves that were strewn across the floor, I would come back later for sure. I raced to my room and managed to get back just as the door slammed shut and sealed itself.

I could see the notice board had updated itself to show the only spell I had not learnt today and the other two I had learnt had vanished completely. I lay down face first on my bed as I contemplated the day, a noise from outside my window startled me and I jumped up to inspect what has caused me such a fright. Outside my window hovering off the ground was Lara but this did not look like the usual Lara, this was just a faint outline of her usual self. I kept on looking and as I did she passed through the solid wall to the side of my window like she was a ghost. I spun around and found her in my room and she spoke out to me 'Joe this is the ghost spell, how amazing is this, my body is in my own room but my soul is here with you. I can go anywhere I want and nobody would even know about it.'

I couldn't believe my eyes, what I was seeing was so cool. I needed to learn this spell then I would have a way of going back and seeing my family, I must have spoken out loud as Lara then told me the downside to the spell, that when in this ghost like state, I would be only able to choose one person to see me and that Lara had chosen that person to be me. If I learnt this spell I knew I would also have to choose Lara as that would only be fair.

The thought of seeing my Mum again was playing on my mind, the possibility was now becoming more of a reality but Lara had insisted that if I learnt this spell, then I was to choose her so we could fool around at night and still see each other. She told me that we could spend more time out of our rooms and in the outside space. She flaunted the idea she even wanted to see the dark gardens and this filled me with dread as a shiver made it's way down my spine. She stayed and chatted with me a little while longer and then explained she needed to get back to her body and that she would meet me at lunch time tomorrow to show me the spell. She passed back through the wall and laughed at my horrified expression. I lay back on my bed and the thought of seeing my Mum again had really lifted my spirits, how would I explain this to Lara. I closed my eyes and drifted off to sleep after an hour or so.

I could hear my name being called and I thought I had not been asleep all that long and it could not be time to get up already. I opened my eyes and realised that I was back in the garden from Uncle Barry's house, I couldn't understand how this had happened and I looked around to see who had been calling my name, there by the back door stood my Mum and I looked over in shock and could not believe this was happening.

I shouted out to my Mum 'How come I'm back here Mum, I don't understand?'

Mum smiled at me and replied,

'Joe you are dreaming, I'm in your dream and this will work all the time now. The silver object you found is a dream tele-porter, when you walked through the door I cast the dream tele-porter through the door to find a way to reach you. You must leave it where you have found it, the magic can only last ten dreams, I will space them out the best I can Joe, but you must know you will be there for years learning magic and becoming powerful enough to end this once and for all.'

My mouth dropped open and a wave of emotion washed over me, my Mum was in my dreams and I would be able to talk to her. I didn't want to wake up and this dream to be over. I told my Mum that I missed them all so very much at this Mum walked over to me and wrapped her arms around me and whispered into my ear, 'I know you will do well Joe and we are all so very proud of you, please don't ever give up, we all miss you dearly but I will come and see you again very soon, I love you so very much son.'

Mum walked back away from me and the dream melted away, I woke suddenly and went to the window and looked outside to see if my Mum was by the dream tele-porter and there was nothing there. I had a feeling of sadness wash over me but this made me more determined to do everything in my power to learn all the spells. I wanted to be even stronger than Lady Malaga, something that night changed me forever.

Chapter 13

SOMETHING'S CHANGED

My room door swung open and I expected to see Blue standing there as usual but there was no sight or sound of him. This was unusual but I told myself that he must already be at breakfast. I exited my room and the door swung shut behind me and I started to wonder what had happened to Blue. I made my way to the breakfast hall and thought I would meet him there. I walked into the breakfast hall but all I could see where red warlocks everywhere and could not see Blue at all. I started to worry about what would of caused his sudden disappearance. I spotted Mrs Green talking to Mr Fire and decided to walk up and ask them both where Blue was. I found myself hearing the end of the conversation and Mrs Green telling Mr Fire that he was to be the one to tell me. I demanded to know where Blue was and Mrs Green whipped her head around to face me and said, 'It's all your fault Joe, she's sent him to the ends of the world and you're entirely to blame.'

I thought I must have still been in my dream and started to laugh and said back to Mrs Green 'You're joking right? Blue has to be here, we have training to do today.'

Mrs Green's face turned a murderous colour of red through the green and she started to wave her arms around 'How dare you laugh about this, this is not a laughing matter, you've caused this you little trouble maker.'

As Mrs Green's anger built her hair started to fire out the silver spikes, they flew all over the place and hit every possible surface, everyone started to dodge out of the way of them. Lara came running towards me and pushed me out of the way, as she did a spike hit her directly in the back and she dropped to the floor screaming and writhing in pain. I turned back to Mrs Green and shouted at her to look what she had done and what she had caused because of her temper. She looked at me with a harrowing expression, casts a spell, apologises and then vanishes. I carried Lara out to the fountain and laid her into the water as she was healing I ran into the centre of the training arena and shouted up to the sky 'How dare you do this you evil being, bring Blue back right now.'

I was so angry Lady Malaga has taken Blue from me I called out her name so many times, then I heard a loud laugh and her face appeared in the sky with the black smoke all around her face 'You don't call me boy, I call you, how dare you demand from me, you bow down to me remember?'

Out of the sky shot a red bot of lightening and it hit me, I could feel myself sink to my knees as she spoke out again 'That's better, you will never see your precious Blue ever again.'

I just had enough energy to shout out back to her 'Please don't do this, I will do whatever you want, please bring Blue back.'

I could see Lara being lifted out of the water and begin to float in mid air and then she spoke out again 'You need to start learning boy, you are mine and I have you now and you will do as I say or I will cast your little friend out as well.' With this she vanished and Lara was dropped back to the ground. Again I had no choice to stop going against Lady Malaga.

I couldn't lose another friend, that was Lara. I ran over to Lara to make sure she was ok, she was fine but in a hurry to get to her next lesson. I could hear my name being called in the distance. I shouted I'm here, I'm Joe. I saw a figure walking towards me and it was a lady with black curly hair in a red jumper, 'Hello Joe my name is Mrs Evil I will be your new trainer.' She smiled with her red eyes.

I told her that I wanted Blue to train me and not her and that was the worst thing I could have said, she just looked at me and said, 'I won't have that kind of attitude Joe, let's get things clear shall we, I have a little lesson that will teach you not to mess with me. Let me see what your greatest fear is.... Ahh yes this will do nicely.'

She cast a spell and it made me see my fear right in front of me, I screamed and nearly passed out. I told her to please make it stop and she said 'That's better Joe we now understand each other don't we? The fear she just showed me was a spider the size of a house, it was just so scary, I had to forget about Blue for now and focus, I miss him so much, I wonder why Lady Malaga cast him out, did she find out that he was showing me the cage spell and that was his punishment? I promised myself there and then I will save him and the all the others that had been punished and cast out.

Mrs Evil doesn't look like she is going to be like Blue by any means and she starts by going through what she will be training me in today. I didn't want to interrupt her so I waited patiently until she addressed me. We started walking to the training ground and she said that she wanted to see what I have learnt already, so without any further delay I cast the first spell that Blue had taught me. She didn't seem that impressed and told me that was a very basic spell and to show her another one, I did the second spell I had learnt and yet again the look of disappointment on her face was evident. She walked up to me and snarled in my face 'So you have only learnt two spells on your first training day, what about any others? Let's see them shall we?'

I told her that Blue had only trained me in those two so far and nothing else, she yelled into my face to stop lying to her and that I must have learnt more by now and demanded that I showed her. I didn't know what to say to her so I came up with the excuse that Blue wasn't feeling too well yesterday and told me to keep practicing the two spells until they were perfect. Mrs Evil gave me the most evil look and screamed into my face 'I've heard it all now, you are just a lazy apprentice, this isn't the place you come to play games, you will be working until I say otherwise, your holidays are over. I am in charge of you now and you will give me 100% every time. By the way, did Blue mention that we can choose the side effects of the spells?'

The way she said this started to worry me a little, thinking she was going to choose some horrible side effect as punishment. I told her that he didn't and she said 'I didn't think so, now show me anything else you can do, anything, it's your choice.'

Did she mean more spells or anything else, the only thing I knew I could do was to touch my nose with my tongue, so I did this and she laughed out loud. She told me that was enough and that she would show me everything I needed to know. Lady Malaga has told me she wants you at your very best and I am the person who will get results no matter what. She explained that I was to watch her very closely as she was going to demonstrate the control spell, she raised her hands towards the sky and began to cast. The spell hit one of the birds that was happily flying through the sky, she stopped the bird in mid air and showed me how she was controlling how the bird flew and all of it's movements. She aimed the bird towards me, laughed and said 'Your turn, stop the bird from hitting you.'

All I could see was this bird winging its way towards me, she was manically laughing and said 'You think it's just the one bird do you? Think again.' I looked beyond the first bird and could see a flock or birds coming towards me, I tried to dodge the birds but she cast another spell at me freezing my legs and stopping me moving. The only option I had was to learn a spell that would stop these birds from knocking me out, I attempted a spell twice and nothing happened. I looked down at my legs and noticed they were turning blue and starting to feel really cold, I knew that Mrs Evil had chosen a cold side effect if I was not going to master this spell. I really concentrated and pushed myself and managed to cast a spell towards the birds and i managed to stop them and even touch one. In anger Mrs Evil turned her anger towards the birds and made them drop from the sky and plunge to the ground. She laughed at me and taunted me by saying 'You want to save the birds do you? Well I know of the spell you created and i know you can't remember it yet, so for now the birds can wait for you until you do remember.'

I can't understand how Mrs Evil could be so evil but her name gave it away, she just killed the birds for no reason, but she was right, I will be able to save them when I remember the spell I created in my past life. She cast all the dead birds over to the dark gardens where she said I can help them once I've completed my training. Her ways were so evil but I was adamant to make things better, Mrs Evil reminded me of a mini Lady Malaga. I wouldn't say that to her because I didn't want to be at the end of that wrath. She wanted to make sure I could master the spell as best I could so then she decided to then control big rocks and they started hurtling through the air at full speed towards me.

Well, let's see how you do now then with the biggest grin on her face. I was still trapped in her spell where I couldn't move and at this point I felt my legs could just break apart with the ice forming. I had to cast quickly as the rocks where mere meters away, I cast out and I stopped the rocks. Mrs Evil shrugged her shoulders and smashed the rocks into pieces with another one of her spells, it looked like she didn't like to be beaten, she released me from the frozen spell. I could only just feel my feet and legs again so she let me go to the water to heal my self, I started to crawl up to the water as my legs just weren't working, I managed to sit on the edge of the fountain and picked up my legs one at a time and submerge them into the water. This had to be the best feeling, my legs and feet started to feel really warm, I looked around at the sound of a laugh and could see a rock heading towards me. I cast out a spell to stop the rock and throw it back towards Mrs Evil. I knew I shouldn't have done that but I couldn't take anymore.

Mrs Evil saw the rock coming towards her, she lifted herself of the ground and with her arms out stretched she cast out and I saw the rock explode. She started to fly towards me and I just wanted the floor to eat me up, she reached me and floated back to the ground and told me that I had done great work and that i was finally understanding her.

Now I was shocked by this as I thought my punishment would have been severe but she appeared to like me fighting back. After that moment I could see a small glint in the eye of Mrs Evil and I knew she had a good sense of humour. She explained that we would be moving onto the last bit now and there would be no more rocks or laughter, I couldn't help but laugh at her comments but something in my head was telling me that she was having a joke with me now but that did not excuse what she did with the birds previously. I would let that go for now as I needed to finish this last lesson. The main difference between Blue and

Mrs Evil was that Blue was friendly and he would never harm anything and would help as much as possible, but Mrs Evil had a dark streak and would like to take things to the extreme to make people learn. She was my teacher now and I knew I would have to do what she said because the side effects and the aftermath were too high a price to pay.

We both walked down to the training arena once again and she says this would be my last spell of the lesson and this would be the disarming spell. She cast a spell and a tree appeared brandishing a sword in its branches, the tree started advancing towards her with the sword swiping through the air. She cast a second spell and the sword that the tree was holding was seized by Mrs Evil who sliced it through the air and it hit the tree with a deathly thunk and the tree was cut in two. I had never seen anything like this before but knew the tree did not stand a chance against Mrs Evil. With a twist of her wrist another tree had formed with another sword, she looked over at me and said 'Your turn.'

She laughed out at me and the ground I was standing on started to sink like quick sand and the tree was heading towards me swiping the sword through the air. My body was falling quicker and quicker through the dirt as I cast and nothing happened. The mud now came up to my waist and the tree was so very close, in the corner of my eye, I saw the sword lift up and coming crashing down, with all my might I cast out one last time and in slow motion i could see the sword just miss me and become under my control. There was no way I could cut a tree in half, so I controlled the sword to the ground. Mrs Evil shouted out and said 'That's not what i wanted, that was boring.'

She began to control the sword again and sliced the tree into bits, she cast me out of the ground and called the days training to an end. She walked off laughing and I could not get over the mentality of her training methods. I started to brush myself down as the dirt was all over my clothes and I heard my name being called and saw it was Lara running towards me.

'Why are you covered in dirt Joe, what have you been up to?' she said smiling at me. I told her that I had a new teacher called Mrs Evil and she looked at me and said 'Oh no you have her, she is the worst teacher with the strictest rules and her side effects for the spells are just really bad.'

'I want to show you the ghost spell, you will love it' I had to choose her to see me as that was our deal, to be fair I can see my Mum in my dreams so that's ok, so I decided that I don't mind if Lara is the person I choose. We went into the gardens a bit further afield somewhere I had never been before. Lara explained she always comes here as it's her relaxing place, I needed to find out a bit more about Lara, what was her background? Where did she live and what was her family was like? I'm looking forward to getting to hang out with Lara where we can use the ghost spell at night for our escape. We entered a place where there were lots of beautiful butterflies flying through the air and rows of fresh apple trees, Lara shows me her spot and it's by a small river. She takes a seat on the ground and puts her feet in the river and tells me to join in. I take a seat next to Lara and she says the spell is so simple Joe, all you have to do is think of calming relaxing thoughts and say release my soul and it's that simple. We can't do it now but we can do it later, all I do is lay in my bed and think of calming thoughts and say the spell so you do the same tonight. 'If we say do this at 8pm sharp, I'll meet you outside Joe. Right Joe, we have to go back to our rooms, the doors will be soon be open and I can't wait to see you later and I know you can do this.'

We both head back to our rooms and there is a butterfly that latched on to me and wouldn't let go so I left it on my shoulder. I entered my room and the door shut, I looked at the notice board and the spells I had learnt went away, I waited to see if anymore appeared but none did. The butterfly that took a liking to me let go and started to flit around my room it then landed on the board. The body of the butterfly started to blend into the board then it became a picture of a butterfly and words started to appear underneath the butterfly.

Welcome all apprentices, congratulations on completing your first stage of the Warlock test, the next test will soon be upon you, each student will have a different insect on their board and yours will be a butterfly. This will mean you have to work towards gaining the power to fly, but as you know before a butterfly blossoms they are in a cocoon. You will need to complete a further two tests to gain the flying spell, this will be up to your trainer to see if this is the right fit for you, good luck.

This is going to be so cool, learning a flying spell. I lay on my bed and could understand why we needed to rest after the Warlock tests and could understand that it wasn't such a bad thing that the door sealed shut. You just had to make sure you did everything before you go to your room like visiting the bathroom. I couldn't wait until 8pm to try the ghost spell with Lara, whilst I was resting all I could think about was how much I had done since seeing the flash of light. It certainly changed my life and I couldn't wait to be a fully trained Warlock. I closed my eyes and started to drift to sleep, I started to see the town where Lady Malaga grew up and thought this was slightly strange as I thought I could only see that if I had drank the tea. The image starts to become clearer and I could see a man in an old looking cottage. All the windows were smashed and the door was hanging off its hinges. I slowly walked up to the door and the image started to become blurry, all I could see was a man casting spells. I tried to get a closer look but the more I tried to focus the worse it got, my head started to hurt really bad and I had to cover my head with my hands. I just kept saying over and over to myself wake up wake up and the image went dark. I started to scream in pain the minute I woke up, I leapt from my bed and my head was still hurting. All I could hear in my ears was a really loud high pitched noise, it got so bad I had to lay back on the bed and wished the pain would go away it got that bad I had to bury my head into the pillow then all of a sudden it went.

I looked at my watch and saw it was nearly time to cast the spell, at this point I just wanted to relax after what had just happened but I promised Lara. I know you need to be in a relaxed calm state for this spell to work and I really wanted to go out into the grounds to explore, ok here goes, come on Joe clear your mind think of happy thoughts. I lay back and think of the lovely things me and my Mum used to do while Dad was away, thinking of the lovely village we lived in and all of the wonderful people. I say the spell just like Lara told me to, I slowly feel my soul lift up out of my body and I look back and there my body was on the bed. It's worked, my soul has come away from my body, this felt creepy but at the same time so cool. I just can't stop looking at my body on the bed, I slowly lift up more and more and suddenly think I'm about to go through the celling and didn't know how to control this spell. I'm moving up through the floorboards and I am now in someone else's room, I try and grab on to something to stop me from floating higher and my hands just go right through anything I grab. I am now moving up more and more through rooms and rooms until I finally realise I am out in the outdoor space in the sky, high off the ground. I hear a shout, it's Lara she says, 'What are you doing all the way up there.' And laughs at me.

I explained that I could not control my movements and whilst still laughing, she tells me that I have to think where I want to go and then my soul works with my thought pattens. I imagine being on the ground and I start descending to where Lara's ghost form awaits me.

I laughed back as this is what I needed right now. I really wanted to tell Lara what had just happened but it would be a long story telling her all about the tea and we didn't have much time. Lara pulls on my arm as she is the only one that can see me and interact with me. She explains that this spell will only last an hour and then we will be back in our bodies, this is only a short spell but I loved using it at night just to feel free again.

I have been in this place for almost two years now, I didn't quite understand how quick time passes in this place and just like that, two years of my life had vanished and i'm still training but almost done. I'm not sure what will happen to me after, everyone says that I'm really good at casting and will make a really good warlock. I still fear that I will be controlled to be the top red for Lady Malaga but I try and not think about it. I like being me, I don't want to be the top red, i'd rather run away, but Lady Malaga would find me and cast me out to the ends of the world. Lara pulls my arm up and we both float into the air she says I'll race you to that apple tree. We were both floating through the air and she beats me to the apple tree. This place must mean something to Lara and I hoped she would tell me. We float back down to the ground where Lara would usually put her feet in the river and she tells me to look at the stars. 'Isn't it nice, check out that big bright one over there,' I look up and it was the brightest star I've ever seen, she says 'That's my Mum there.' She tells me she misses her so much and that she lost her Mum when she was younger. She was taken by a red warlock but she was told that her Mum had fallen down some stairs and didn't make it. Only when she grew up did she learn the truth, she wanted to become a warlock herself and to find the warlock that killed her Mum. This was very sad and I had tears in my eyes, Lara told me not to cry as she didn't cry and she needed to be strong. We chatted for a little bit more and by the time Lara had told me about her Mum it was almost time for the spell to wear off. She told me that before we went that she needed to show me something quickly, I was intrigued with what Lara wanted to show me, she started to float up in the air and she said come with me. She went so fast but I caught up with her and we ended up by the dark gardens and my heart skipped a beat.

'Don't be scared Joe we're not going in, I just wanted to show you.' She says

I sighed with relief as just looking at the dark gardens made me go all funny.

'Joe the spell is going to wear off, same time tomorrow, yeah?' she says.

Before I knew it I was back in my room tucked up in bed. This magic was great and I couldn't believe my luck. Who would of thought I would be learning the warlock secrets and coming face to face with an evil witch. This was something you would read about in a book but not happen to me. I just hoped Lara was ok with opening up to me like that, I really felt for her but she didn't want me to show any emotion towards her and I respected that. I just hoped Mrs Evil will be nice to me tomorrow when learning my new spells, how cool will it be to fly. I begin to wonder what Mrs Evil will choose for me to complete my test of flying, I hope it's not really bad.

Closing my eyes I just imagined what it was going to be like flying with the spell, will it give me wings or will i just fly through the air like the dreaded Lady Malaga? What's that noise I can hear? I look up to the celling and there was the butterfly again, it was so beautiful, the wings were so colourful with blue and purple strips. I can see it just looking at me it started to fly down towards me, the wings were just so mesmerising and I fell into a trance. My eyes were so heavy but I could slightly open them, I saw the butterfly right in front of my face the wings beating so fast it made me close my eyes again. I could hear a slight voice echo around me it was so relaxing, the voice must be coming from the butterfly. I listened intently to the voice and I could make out someone introducing themselves to me.

'Hello Joe, my name is Mr Butter, don't laugh, they gave my name to me as a nick name for butterfly. I'm here as I'm your chosen warlock partner, all warlocks have them, you are in for a treat Joe, not only am I a butterfly but I can also take you places, watch this.'

As Mr Butter kept on talking I opened my eyes and noticed that everything about Mr Butter was growing along with everything in my room. The window in my room now filled the entire wall and Mr Butter himself was now a giant butterfly. What had happened? Was I dreaming yet again? As I thought this, Mr Butter spoke out again.

'See Joe, you now can jump on my back and I can take you anywhere, this is one of the powers you have while having me by your side. You can also shrink so no one can see you and I am here for that anytime. This is just the beginning Joe, we are going to be the best of friends.'

This is fantastic I can shrink anytime, I was beginning to think that this couldn't get any better. I ran up to Mr Butter and jumped on his back and he took off flying around the room. The view of my room looked so strange but I was loving it, wait a minute, how do I summon you if I need you Mr Butter? 'Joe all you have to do is call my name and I'll be there for you.'

So if I'm in danger I can call Mr Butter how cool was that. I was flying around for about 10 minutes getting used to this and then Mr Butter says he has to go and that I can only call him if I need him. I said goodbye to Mr Butter and I was back to my normal size and fell into bed. All of the flying around made me very tired and I needed to be ready for my test tomorrow.

Chapter 14

LEARNING TO FLY

I startled awake and opened my eyes to a loud voice shouting my name from outside my room. It was loud enough to wake the whole headquarters up and I just wanted to cover my head with my pillow and sink back into the mattress. I knew this would never be allowed, i got up and walked over to the door and I recognised the voice instantly as the shivers crept down my spine. The voice belonged to Mrs Evil, she shouted through the door,

'You better be ready for today Joe, I have a special treat for you. Do you think you are worthy to have the flying spell? If so you will have to work really hard, starting out with no breakfast.'

She then banged on the door which made me jump out of my skin and also warned me not to let her down or be late and that she would see me outside in thirty minutes sharp. She banged on the door again to make her point clear and well known and marched off. I didn't understand why I wasn't allowed any breakfast and I knew I had to prove Mrs Evil wrong. I would get that flying spell, even if it was the last thing I did. I began to reflect on what had happened last night with the arrival of Mr Butter, did the other warlocks here have their partner or was it just me? I knew he and I would get on really well and would have a right laugh with each other. I knew the door would momentarily open, so I started hunting for my shoes. Where the hell had they gone and why couldn't I find them? I couldn't believe my bad luck as time ticked away growing ever towards when I would be late. I searched high and low and still could not find them so I made the daring decision and grabbed one of the books from the shelf, hoping that there would be a spell to conjure up some shoes. I was in luck as the book opened on the page of the shoe summoning spell, and it came with a warning.

Warning: The shoe summoning spell will bring a pair of shoes to life. Please be warned, these shoes will have their own mind and desire and love to mess around. Choose wisely as they can cause mayhem.

I had no other choice as I needed a pair of shoes and I couldn't be late. It wasn't going to be that bad surely, the spells in these books were very simple for beginners, so I couldn't go wrong. Right, here goes, I began to cast the spell with my ring and said the spell,

'Shoes on my feet, shoes on my feet, I need you now to make me complete.'

It worked and a pair of shoes materialised at the end of my bed, I quickly put them on and ran outside as soon as my door opened. I made it to the training ground just in the nick of time as Mrs Evil was standing there with her arms crossed. I was ready for whatever she was going to throw my way today. She told me that I had to complete two spells before she would give me the flying spell, she laughed and hoped that I was ready. I told her I was. As we began to work I could feel a slight tickling on the bottom of my feet and this was making me laugh out. Mrs Evil stared down at me and shouted 'What is so funny? I do not allow this behaviour in my class.'

The tickling continued and I just burst of laughing time and time again, Mrs Evil warned me to stop or else there would be consequences. The tickling stopped and I got up a little red faced and embarrassed from all of the laughter. The shoes did come with a warning but I decided to go against the warning and now I was facing the mayhem that they would surely cause. I tried to forget about the shoes as I did not want to upset and face the wrath of Mrs Evil. She walked up to me and grabbed hold of my ear and issued a warning 'Any funny business in my class again and you will be sent to Warlock jail for a whole day and night, where you can reflect on your misdemeanours. Trust me boy, that place is vile even for me. It's pitch black with not one ray of daylight and spiders crawl over your skin, oh and did I mention that the roof leaks so water drips on you continuously for the whole of your stay.'

I nodded back to her to show my understanding, she walked back to the centre of the training grounds and resumed casting the first spell I would be learning. This would be the spell to defeat my enemies, she cast hundreds upon hundreds of mushrooms that surrounded her, I remembered seeing this before, she showed me just the one time how to defeat them and then turned to me and said your turn. This time she cast a lot more mushrooms and these again surrounded me, these were not the small mushrooms you would imagine but large and very dangerous. If these touched you then you would become very ill. Mrs Evil spoke out and said 'Let's see what you've got then shall we?'

She started to laugh as the mushrooms started to charge towards me, I cast out towards the mushrooms and as I defeated them, she cast more and more of them to take the others place. I didn't stand a chance against them and just when I thought all hope was lost, my ring started to glow and got really bright. Suddenly, a beam of light shot out of my ring and spun around all of the mushrooms and destroyed them all. I looked over at Mrs Evil with a look of triumph of my face, I could see that a look of shock had painted itself on her face. She shouted out 'This cannot be, you cannot be him.'

She lowered into a bow in front of me and would not get up until her nose was nearly touching the ground. Why was she bowing to me? She looked back at me and asked if it was really me. I didn't know what she meant by this and I still did not understand why she was bowing to me. She explained to me that they had been waiting a very long time for a very strong warlock to save them all and that no one had seen this Warlock for years. We would be able to sense the magic when it was performed and she told me that she had just sensed this magic. She went on to apologise for being so evil and laughed about it. She told me that she had so much heartache and that no one had really liked her, which had caused her to be bullied when growing up. I could see her expression start to change and could sense her heart start to grow warm towards me.

She told me that I would have to walk across hot coals and master a spell that would allow me not to feel the pain and walk across the coals without any damage at all. Mrs Evil cast out and a section of the training ground transformed into burning hot coals, I could feel the heat coming out from the coals. Mrs Evil told me that she believed in me and knew that I could do it. That coming from her filled me with confidence and meant a lot to me. I took off my shoes and raised my foot over the top of the coals. I suddenly felt a burning sensation start to flick at my feet. I cleared my mind and lowered my feet onto the coals. I looked down and could not believe that I was walking across hot coals and that I could not feel my feet. I walked across the whole section of the coals and once I had got to the other side, I collapsed on the ground as I could not feel my feet. Mrs Evil came over and knelt by my side and told me that I had done it. Mrs Evil went on to explain that the coals were an illusion to see if I was worthy of the flying spell. I looked back at the coals that Mrs Evil had summoned and could see a stream of water in its place. I had passed her tests after all and I felt the pride swell within my chest. Mrs Evil cast a second spell and a pure yellow gem materialised out of thin air. It floated towards me and latched itself onto my ring. Mrs Evil said 'Well done Joe, you've earned that.'

I asked her if I could now perform the flying spell as the excitement flooded my body. She explained that all I had to do was to think of flying and this would happen, I was told about the rules that come with the flying spell. I would not be allowed to fly out of the headquarters as this would come with dire consequences. Lady Malaga likes us grounded, we can only use this spell when we are with her as part of her army. I promised that I wouldn't use this as I didn't want to get the new and improved Mrs Evil into trouble.

We called it a day and Mrs Evil, if you could call her that now, let me go to lunch. As I walked away from the training ground towards the lunch hall, my shoes got really heavy and I could hardly lift them off the ground to make another step. I suddenly heard a laugh and looked around and could see no one that the laughter belonged too. The voice then shouted 'Out over here, I'm here.' I looked down and noticed that my shoes now had a pair of eyes and a mouth. Was I seeing this right or was this another illusion, the voice spoke out again and told me not to be scared and that I was in the Warlock world after all.

My shoes kept saying thank you and explained that he was saying thank you for me casting the spell. He had been trapped within the book for so long and as I cast the spell, it had partially freed him. My shoes went on to tell me that Lady Malaga transformed him into a spell to be trapped in the book until someone freed him. He told me that his name was Ned and that he had been wishing for years that someone would cast the spell that would free him. He said that all he needed now would be for Lady Malaga to be defeated and then his curse would be broken forever. I couldn't believe this was happening, I was now wearing talking shoes called Ned and I began to question if I was slowly losing my mind.

He told me that we have to make a move towards the dark gardens and I thought to myself that there was no way I would be going there, not a chance. Ned speaks out and says 'I think you are going Joe, did I forget to mention that I can hear your thoughts and read your mind, there is no point in thinking you can take me off your feet either.'

Ned started to control my feet and we started to walk towards the dark gardens, I needed to stop this from happening, but I could not move my own feet as he had complete control of me, I now understand the warning fully, I had done something that I shouldn't have.

'That's right Joe you have, I'm sorry to disturb your thoughts right now but I don't have time for this, I hear you have just mastered the flying spell Joe, I can also control your mind, get ready for take off.'

I told Ned to stop as we are not allowed to fly in headquarters.

'Do you do everything you're told Joe get ready, hope you can fly well Joe.'

I could feel my feet starting to lift off the ground, I tried so hard to force my feet to stay on the ground but it was no good, Ned has got control of my mind, the ground started to disappear as I lifted off. As we were flying through the air, Ned speaks out, '

'Let's see you fly Joe, we will do a couple of practice loops round the grounds before we head off.'

I shouted at Ned to stop and I knew this would cause attention. Ned laughed and said people would think I was crazy as he was just a pair of shoes and could hide when he needed to. Ned makes me fly another two laps of the grounds and I could see some of the red Warlocks doing training. They couldn't see what was going on as they were busy. I spotted Lara and Ned warns me about making too much noise as I would get into trouble.

We were heading towards the dark gardens and my heart was racing, I could have almost passed out in a panic, I come up with a plan quickly and thought about calling Mr Butter. Ned asks who is Mr Butter as I had forgotten he could read my thoughts. I didn't reply and I called out to him to come and rescue me. I shouted out zoom me and I began to shrink. I climb onto the back of Mr Butter and say for him to take me to my room. Ned repeatedly tried to make me fly off the butterfly's back but I held on for dear life. Ned told me I was making a big mistake, I flew back over the training grounds and into my room, I asked for the butterfly to keep flying around my room until the door sealed shut, this way I knew Ned would not be able to make me leave again. As the door slammed shut, I returned to my original size and I thanked Mr Butter for his help. Ned began to squeeze my feet really tight in his fit of anger but eventually gave up and sighed 'I needed to go to the dark gardens as my sister is there, I needed to make sure she was ok, it's been years since we've both seen each other and I believe some dark magic has got her. The last time we saw each other we both got split up.'

I gave Ned the chance to tell me his story as I wanted to know more of what had happened. He told me that years ago his sister and he were very close and that they would do everything together. We liked to help each other and of course other people, we had such good times with each other and loved working in this place until Lady Malaga took over. He told me he couldn't remember much about that ill fated day apart from the screams that filled his mind every time he tried to rest. He told me that Lady Malaga had cast a spell on both him and his sister, the spell forced them into a spell book for eternity or until someone found the exact spell and cast, their souls were forced to be trapped in the dark gardens. He explained that he was trying to save his sister and all those that had been trapped and would do anything to make his mission a success. He made a plea to me for help but warned me about the army of trees that guarded the edge of the dark garden.

That's why Ned was taking me there, I fully understood now and I knew I must help him, I'm the one who would need to come up with a plan. I knew that the dark gardens were so dangerous and that if we set foot there, I'm sure Lady Malaga would do something about it.

Ned spoke out and I forgot he can read my mind. We needed to get a plan together, I felt like I wanted to involve Lara in this. If we did the ghost spell at night we could really see what we were going to face in the dark gardens. I thought about using Mr Butter but I needed to be at my full size as I wouldn't be able to do anything.

'Joe I have a plan.' says Ned.

'Yes go ahead what is it?' I answer back.

'I know in one of the spell books you have that there is a magic spell that can make you invisible. But this will only last thirty minutes then the spell is broken. After the first thirty minutes, you can't use it again, it could get us in the dark gardens but it can't get us out that's the problem.'

It sounded like a good plan but I needed to find a way to get us back out. We needed to check what was in there first, with the ghost spell I could fly over there and check it out, but I would need to tell Lara. Ned tells me that wouldn't be a problem as long as she did not tell anyone else. I would have to speak with her and do the ghost spell tonight. Ned explained that he couldn't take any chances of Lady Malaga finding out. The plan sounded like it could work, I made a mental note to meet with Lara later and explain everything and make her promise not to say a word. I knew Lara was close to completing her training or for that matter turning into a red Warlock and possibly dropping us into trouble with the dreaded Lady Malaga.

I started to think about dinner and wondered what the delights would be this evening and was getting hungry thinking about it all. My door opened and I marched across the grounds and made my way into the dinner hall. Ned kept talking about his sister the whole way across to dinner and I reassured him that we would find her and save her. Dinner smelt good for a change and I caught sight of Lara walking towards me, I shouted for her to join me in line as I had something to tell her, but she said she couldn't as she was in a hurry as Lady Malaga had requested her presence after dinner. I asked why she was going to see Lady Malaga and Lara explains that she has been summoned but she was unsure why. As she carried on walking, she spun around and said 'I can't do tonight if you catch my drift.' And walked off.

I wondered what Lady Malaga wanted with Lara and I was a little worried. Will Lara open her mouth and tell her all the stuff we have done already? This could turn out quite bad, but I trusted Lara and hoped she would stay quiet. I was going to have to wait and see what would come out of their meeting. Ned told me to forget about everything and eat as I would need the strength. As I got to the front of the line, I could see dinner was stew and crusty bread. I filled up my bowl and made my way to sit down to eat. I could feel the stew warming up my insides as I chowed down. I got back to my room after dinner and looked out the spell book that would help with our adventure to the dark gardens.

I asked Ned to release my feet from the shoes so I could rest for a little bit and he obliged but did say I was stuck with him until he was free from his curse and his sister had been saved. I looked through the book for the spell I would need, I found the spell really odd and attempted to get my head around it but I just could not figure it out. I dropped the book and told Ned I needed to get some sleep. A message appeared on my notice board telling me the spell I would learn tomorrow and I thought this could come in handy for our little planned adventure. It was the illusion spell and was warned that the side affects could be horrific if I failed this test and also that this was the toughest test I would face. I knew I needed to get some rest ready for the day ahead. I said goodnight to Ned and fell into a deep settled sleep.

Chapter 15

BLUES BACK

'Wake up sleepy head wake up' Ned shouts at me, I opened my eyes and the shoes were already on my feet, I was still in bed but Ned didn't like that so he made me roll out of bed and hit the ground with a thump. He laughed and thought it was so funny. He says,

'Come on Joe, we have to get out to the training grounds, it's the big one today the illusion spell, you will love this. I know I did when I was training.'

I picked my mouth up from the shock of learning that Ned was a Warlock and he told me to get a move on as he hated being trapped in this room after the years of being trapped in a book. My door sprung open and Ned made me dash all the way to the training grounds, we were going that fast I expected smoke to come off the shoes at any minute. We made it down to the training grounds and as usual, there stood Mrs Evil she asked if I was ready for today after I told her I was, she began to cast out and I watched her intently. Suddenly a massive alligator appeared, I screamed out in a panic and Mrs Evil, told me to stop being silly as this was not real. She walked up to the alligator and tapped it on the head. She cast again and again and more alligators appeared. She explained that this was the illusion spell and this could be used to trick your opponents in order to give you some more time to make your mind up as to what you were going to do. She told me that the lesson and test would be difficult but she had every faith in my abilities.

I just nodded my head, she shouted for me to watch her again and cast at the same time. I watched everything Mrs Evil did and attempted to do the same but nothing happened I did it again and still nothing happed. Mrs Evil didn't look impressed and she shouted 'Watch like this Joe.'

I followed her again, but nothing happened, by this point Mrs Evil looked fed up and she said 'One more time Joe, come on you can do this I know you can.'

I cast again then something happened, I looked over and there were four Mrs Evil's looking at me. They were all fighting about who was the real one and who was an illusion. I had to choose the real Mrs Evil. I kept looking at all of them, they were all doing the same things as each other. It was really difficult, I walked towards them and the ground started to feel slippery, I looked down and a mirror had formed. I looked back up and there were hundreds of Mrs Evil's everywhere the whole training ground had become a gigantic mirror, this was making my mind go all funny.

All the Mrs Evil's were still arguing at the same time saying 'I'm the real one, no I am, I'm over here.'

I just looked in every direction and I couldn't make out which was the real Mrs Evil, I suddenly remember what I have learnt and I let my sense of feeling be drawn to the real Mrs Evil. As I walked towards her, all the others started to fade away and as I got up close to Mrs Evil I knew I had picked the right one. She said 'Well done Joe you did it.'

The mirrors started to melt away and there was the training ground again. I was glad at this point as I don't think I could take any more of the mirrors, my eyes were a little hazy from all of the shiny glass. I looked around and couldn't believe my eyes. It can't be! Is it! In the distance walking up to me there was Blue. I could have cried there and then. He shouted out to me 'Joe my friend, you have done so well with your training.'

I couldn't find the words to speak as I ran towards him to give him the biggest cuddle ever. I said 'Blue I can't believe it, how are you here? I thought you were cast out?'

He replied 'Well Joe, you know me, you can't get rid of me that easily.'

I let go of Blue and stood back and he started to laugh, out came a higher pitched laugh and then he was lifted off the ground into mid air, the Blue I knew started to change colour and then there was black smoke circling around him. I was just in shock by this, the laughter died down and he spoke out.

'You foolish boy, did you really think that Blue would be back, you're more stupid than I ever thought possible, you will never see Blue again.'

I was so angry that I shouted back 'You're evil, where's Blue?'

'Quiet, you will give me what I want, even if I have to wait years. Now get back to training, I will say hello to Blue from you.'

The smoke covered up what I thought was Blue, then Lady Malaga's face appeared with her cackling like the old witch that she was and then disappeared. I put my head in my hands then lifted up my head and let out a loud scream, I was so upset as I really thought that was Blue. Mrs Evil saw how upset I was but she didn't know what to say to me to make me feel any better. I just took my mind off the training and I took myself away. Mrs Evil was ok with this and told me to come back in thirty minutes. I needed to clear my mind and calm down and be fresh for my training, she wants me to pass, this spell would be so handy to have. I walked over to the other side of the training ground and found a nice spot on a rock just thinking, I forgot Ned could hear my thoughts and he tried to cheer me up by telling me a few jokes which were really bad, but I just wasn't in the mood to laugh. It was nearly time to head back to training but I wasn't moving and then my feet started to walk, it was Ned's doing.

'Come on Joe, don't give up you have got to get this spell, you have to do this for Blue. When you are a fully trained Warlock which I know you will be, didn't you say you wanted to be the most powerful Warlock? Well it starts here, pick yourself back up.'

Those words just changed everything, Ned's right I have to carry on, I raced back to the training ground and told Mrs Evil that I was ready for anything she could and would throw at me, Joe is back and he's staying!

'That's more like it Joe, fighting talk, I like it.' I forgot that Ned could hear my thought and with this I started to laugh.

Mrs Evil cast out a spell again and this time four doors appeared, now I've seen this before and I didn't want to pick the wrong door. I didn't want to go back like last time, think Joe think. I have to get this right, I walked to the second door and I felt a good feeling from this door, Mrs Evil speaks out 'Well don't just stand in front of it open it'

I reached my hand out to the handle shaking while doing this, I grabbed it and pulled it down, the door opened and Mrs Evil told me to walk through. I slowly walked through and the door shut behind me, it made me jump. It was dark in front of me and I started to walk and hit something, the door opened behind me and I turned around and there was Mrs Evil clapping and shouting out, well done Joe you got it right. I walked out feeling so pleased with myself and headed to Mrs Evil. She praised me and said 'Here is the illusion spell.' She cast a ring stone and it floated towards me in the air and latched on to my ring. This was just an amazing feeling, knowing that not many students got this spell. She told me that I just have to say create an Illusion and think of what I want to create.

All of a sudden I was jumping up and down, I looked down at Ned and he was smiling at me, Mrs Evil looked over in shock but gave a little laugh as she walked away. I've completed the test and I am becoming a Warlock, this brought a great smile on my face. I said thank you to Ned for the celebrations but please stop as it's beginning to hurt my legs. He just laughed while saying he was just so happy for me that I passed, he also said we needed to prepare for tonight for when we fly to the dark gardens. I headed back to my room, whilst walking back I saw Lara, she looked at me and carried on walking, I shouted to her and got no response. I ran up to her and she quickly turned towards me, this was not the Lara I knew and loved. I knew Lady Malaga had done something, she spoke out and said 'You really want to work harder Joe for what's about to come.'

And with that she walked off, what did that mean what had Lady Malaga got planned?

This was really bothering me now, Ned told me that I needed to forget about her she's turned you won't get through to her. I didn't want to believe that, there must be a way to get her back. As I headed back to my room, a girl I had never seen before ran towards me, she knew a lot about me and that she was also friends with Lara, she was called Kathy but liked to be called Kat. She told me that she knows that something is up with Lara and that she caught her doing all sorts of spells the other day and that she nearly got caught. She told me that she was working beside Lady Malaga, she warned me about tonight and that I shouldn't do what I was going to do, I thought to myself how does she know? She then ran off shouting back ' I've said too much already.'

I entered my room with a big decision to make, do I do the ghost spell or not? I was pacing up and down thinking about this and Ned kept saying to me over and over that I have to, I have to help him but how did Kat know what I was going to do? This was so strange as I've never even seen her and Lara has never talked about Kat before. Ned speaks out to me and says, 'You have to Joe, you said you will help me, I thought we were friends?'

Ned is right I did say I would help him, I can't let him down, I have to do this, I have to help him and his sister. We waited until the evening and I wasn't hungry at all so I missed dinner and waited for the right time. My door was sealed shut now so this was my time to do the spell. Something on the board appeared I thought it was another magic spell I would be learning tomorrow but this was different, it was a message that said 'All apprentices must attend outside on the training ground in ten minutes, the doors will be open, don't be late.'

This has just messed up my evening to explore the dark gardens, Ned wasn't at all happy with this but he said he understood and would let me go. The ten minutes was up and the doors opened, I walked out of my room and people were running and shouting in horror, I thought to myself something wasn't right. I saw Mrs Evil rushing up towards the training ground along with Mr Fire and all the top reds, it was utter mayhem. I walked slowly towards the training ground where everyone was gathered. Suddenly the ground started to shake and there was a black cloud of smoke, everyone stood back, they all knew it was Lady Malaga coming. We were right, the black smoke got much bigger, there was a clap of thunder and she appeared touching down on the training ground. She was dressed in a black and gold long dress, I had never seen anything like it before, it was mesmerising. She cast out a spell that brought out the spell book that I had seen many times before, but this time, it was the size of a car that was standing upright. It glowed so brightly it was almost like the sun, she spoke out to all of us and said,

'Thank you for joining me on this fine evening, I'm here as some of you have broken the rules of my headquarters, I had high hopes for you but clearly I was wrong.'

Everyone's faces just dropped and everyone began to look at each other, Lady Malaga started to walk towards some people. The dress just flowed behind her and the gold started to form into ropes as they began to come from her dress, she spoke out again.

'You have broken the rules, how dare you disobey me!'

The gold ropes unlatched off the dress and moved across the ground like snakes and started to wrap themselves around one of the reds. It picked the girl that I knew was Kat, she was lifted off the ground by the ropes. She attempted to move but the ropes were too tight for her, they started to bring Kat towards Lady Malaga, Lady Malaga just laughed and said 'You will pay for the rules you have broken my dear.'

Lady Malaga cast out a spell, this was the spell that would take the soul out of the body, you could see the soul coming out of the body floating besides Kat in mid air, Lady Malaga cast the soul to the same place she had sent the others, then Kat's body was pulled inside the spell book. Everyone looked on in horror and stayed silent apart from one person Mr Fire. He shouted out at Lady Malaga and said, 'She didn't do anything wrong, how could you, you're nothing but an evil witch. I've had enough of you and your rules, no more!'

Lady Malaga was outraged by this and the ropes of her dress reached for Mr Fire and grabbed him and pulled him closer to Lady Malaga, she grabbed hold of him and said, 'You've got guts I give you that, you will not be going anywhere Mr Fire, in fact you will stay here for ever.'

She continued to laugh and Mr Fire looked on in shock and couldn't believe that she wasn't going to cast him out, he had thought his time was up, but as she let go of his body, it started to turn very slowly into stone. Once the transformation was complete she cast him to stay by the fountain for all eternity, held forever within his stoney prison.

'Anyone that disobeys me, will be added into my spell book, remember you work for me and must obey my rules. You will be my army. Do I make myself clear? The time will come when the world will beg at my feet for mercy.'

She continued to laugh really loudly as she cast out another spell, there was a beam of light so bright it caused the ground to shake and then she was gone just leaving her laughter echoing behind.

Everyone headed back to their rooms and no one spoke, it was silent everywhere. I looked over by the water fountain and there was Mr Fire all in stone, Ned didn't say nothing to me we were just all so sad with what Lady Malaga just done. I really thought that there might be little hope in there for Lady Malaga, but she was just pure evil no one would dare take her on, but I have to do something I have to save all these people and the world, I am their only hope, I must become the most strongest and powerful Warlock.

Chapter 16

THE MESSAGES

I sat on my bed wondering if I could be the one to stop Lady Malaga and started to doubt myself. I took off my shoes as Ned was just too angry to talk but he knew that the time wasn't right to check out the dark gardens. It was too risky because of what had just happened. All I wanted to do was sleep and even leave this place but no that wasn't an option. The best next thing was to dream and get out of this place for a while. I lay back on the bed and started to daydream. As I did my eyes started to get heavy and I drifted off into a deep sleep. This is where I wanted to be, away from that dreaded place, I looked around and I recognised this place, it's where I would come with Mum and Dad to have a break. It was the most beautiful place with high cliffs covered in flowers. Trees dotted along a running stream that spread into the sea, there was a bench in the distance we could sit on and watch the world go by. I walked over to the bench on my own and noticed there were lots of notes on the ground and one was hanging from a tree. The note that was hanging from the tree got caught in the breeze and nearly hit the stream, I ran over to the note and grabbed it and tore it open.

Dear Joe, I'm sorry I can't be with in your dream but I left you this note in the hope that it reaches you. Your Dad and I are so proud of what you are doing. You have to be strong, you are the one everyone has been waiting for. Things haven't always been perfect in our life but having you was the best day of my life. I knew that when you were born you were special and the world would know who you are, keep doing what you're doing, you'll be home very soon. Love Mum.

The note just made me so sad, I saw another note hanging from the tree, it was quite high up and I would have to climb to get it. I knew that I was dreaming and nothing could hurt me, but I was still scared as the wind had started to pick up. I took the first step onto the tree trunk and pulled myself up using one of the branches. I managed to get half way up the tree, I needed that note so I climbed higher and higher, the note blew onto the very last branch that was stretched far out. I would have to climb higher and then lean over with my arms out stretched. At this point I knew someone was testing me. I didn't let the height and the wind stop me, I leant over and grabbed the note and leant back in before the branch snapped clean off. I climbed back down the tree and sat beside the tree reading the note.

Joe my son, if you are reading this note you are stronger than you think, you will be the most powerful Warlock and you just proved it by reaching out for this note. Sorry but you have to be tested, we believe in you Joe and you will do great, love Dad.

Something blew towards me and it was another note, I stood up and the note just blew right by my feet. I picked up the note it was from the other Joe.

Hi bro, hope you're well, all good is here, don't worry about school no one has figured it out so all is sound this end, keep up the good work, we can't wait for you to return home. Thanks again for not letting me go, I didn't understand at first but now I do, Uncle Barry says hello you know what Uncle Barry is like. All the best, Joe your bro.

As I folded the notes to put them into my pocket, the dream started to fade, I was hoping I could stay a little longer. Before I knew it I was out of my dream and I woke up with the biggest smile on my face. I could hear something rattling by the window, I got up and there were all the notes from my dream flying on the wind. I couldn't believe that the notes had become real, I grabbed them holding on to them tightly. Out of the blue another note flew into my room from under my door, it caught my eye as soon as it passed into my room. I picked it up and sat on the bed, I opened the note and it was another one from my Mum, this brought a tear in my eye.

Joe, you might be wondering what is going on after your dream and finding out that these notes are real. The dream spell I cast means that I can leave notes to reach you. I can't see what you're doing but I am feeling that you are doing really well, but don't let that stop you thinking you're out of the woods my son. The time will soon come when you will make the biggest decision in your life. As you know, with this spell I can only cast ten and the notes do class as me coming into your dream, so I want to use this wisely. Remember Joe, we all love you very much, don't stop believing in yourself, you are very special and very strong, you will soon know this yourself. Love Mum.

This is just amazing not only having the messages from my dream but also the messages coming to life, I got off the bed and I reached for one of the spell books. I placed the notes inside the book as I couldn't be caught having them in my room. I thought this when my shoes went missing but it all worked out well as I got to meet Ned the talking shoes. No one would believe me if I said this to my old school friends. I suddenly think about Beck, I hope she is ok, I hope her parents have calmed down a bit on her, she's such a lovely person and would help out anyone if they needed it. I wondered how she was getting on with my twin brother, what if she noticed something was up? Just having these messages brings back memories of home life and everyone. I also remembered the time that Becks wrote to me when she was away with her family camping. She had had the worst time, she was just sitting around in their tent with no contact from anyone, she just wished the days away. The only time she had a bit of fun was when the board games came out in the evening. She was away for two weeks and she wrote to me the first two days into their holiday, she wanted to stay with me, but her family weren't having any of it. I felt so sorry for her when she packed her stuff up in the car, she waved to me from the back seat with a tear in her eye. She couldn't wait to come back. The day she returned, she ran up to my house and we played against each other on my racing game, it was our favourite thing to do. I tried not to think about that now as I didn't want to worry myself, maybe I could ask Mum in my dream next time. I looked at my watch and noticed that the time was getting late, I should really try and get some rest. There were no messages on my board about any training lessons and I wondered what tomorrow would bring. I laid back and started to relax my mind and prayed that I could get to sleep, there was so much going around in my head now but I needed to relax.

Bang!! I woke up out of my relaxed sleep, I was still half asleep when there was another bang!! I sat bolt upright, adjusting my eyes to the dark in the room. I looked everywhere to see what had caused the bang, and there was nothing I could see. I slowly leaned back into my pillow and another bang!! I jumped out of bed my feet banged against a book on the floor, this was odd because all the books should be on the shelves. It can't be the wind as there were no windows open. I turned on the light and all of the books were on the floor, one of the books was wide open and this was the book that I hid the notes in, they were gone!

I scrambled around and lifted up all the books to see if my notes were underneath, there was no sign of the notes at all, this was really strange, just like I couldn't find my shoes. What is going on? Who was in my room taking my stuff? I checked one more place to see if the notes had blown under the bed, I kneeled down to look under the bed and I could see in the very back in the corner two eyes looking at me, this made me jump out of my skin, banging my head in the progress. I sat back up shaking, what was under my bed? I pushed myself again to have another look, there it was just looking at me. What was it I said to myself? I found the words to say hello, who are you and what are you doing under my bed? The eyes were just in a dark shadow I couldn't make out what it was, then the eyes looked like they were getting closer, it turned out the eyes were moving more and more towards me, part of me wanted to move back but I kept really still. At this point something was walking closer and closer until I could see an outline coming out from the shadows.

Then there was a voice that spoke out to me and said, 'Joe don't be scared my name is Silver Lion, I have come to tell you I have taken your shoes and letters to keep them safe, I'm no threat.'

Silver Lion came closer to me and I could see why his name was Silver Lion, he looked just like a small lion but silver. I went to go closer to him but he rolled up into a ball in fright, I moved back and he slowly unravelled himself and spoke out and said 'I'm sorry about that I get scared and that's my way of protecting myself.'

He finally came out from under the bed and walked up close to me. It was so amazing, the silver all over him and his piercing blue eyes, he wanted to show me something that I had to keep a secret. Where I could hide all my important stuff away from Lady Malaga? He said follow me, he walked back under the bed and to my amazement he pointed to the floor where there was a black hole, he spoke out and said 'This hole here is a secret hiding place Joe, sorry that I took your letters but I didn't want you to get caught so I've kept them in a safe place, also this hole can transport you anywhere you want to go in the headquarters grounds.'

By this time I was a bit confused about how this will work. He told me that it's a hiding place for my stuff but also it would transport me anywhere. I had to find out what he meant so I asked, 'How do I choose where I want to go and how can I hide my things without anyone knowing?'

He explained that he would show me if I would follow him. He walked up to the hole and it almost sucked him in. I was a bit nervous about this but I had to find out for myself, I followed him and I was pulled straight down the hole, it was all black then suddenly it became all light and clear. I could see signs appearing, it would stop you at different signs where there was a door you could open, this will lead you to different parts of the headquarters, this was so strange as you could look into the different areas but you were behind a glass where you could see through but nobody could see you, this was so good to know what was gong on without being seen.

Sliver lion showed me all the different parts I could go to, but the only one he didn't have access to was the hideout of Lady Malaga, he had been trying for so many years to find it, but not him or anyone else knew where it was. I only just remembered I was maybe in her hideout before I got transferred to the headquarters. He then showed me where my letters were they were behind a door saying 'Joe's Hideout.'

I couldn't believe this was my own hideout, I opened the door and inside were so many different things belonging to me from when I was young. This all made sense as I used to lose things but I didn't know it had been taken from me for safe keeping. Silver Lion had been watching me all these years! There was one drawing, I had a dream then I drew my dream, this brought back a memory, it was of a lady all in black, maybe I knew from a young age of Lady Malaga but had just forgotten.

'Joe, this is a place where you can get away and look at the memories you have had, they are all here. This will help you become much stronger and fight to carry on, also you can sneak around the headquarters without being caught. Lady Malaga doesn't know about this, and she can never find out.'

I saw a sign saying 'The Training Ground!' I opened the door and there was a full size view of the ground where we do all the training. Shame I can't use this place in the day spying on all of the Warlocks! I then thought to myself I must get to know a lot more of the Warlocks, if i'm going to be here for a while I need to make more friends. I then started to think about Lara as I haven't seen much of her, and i wondered how she was doing. I wondered if I could use this place to check on Lara? But this may not be a good idea as the Silver Lion said not to use this in the day time, I couldn't risk this place being found out.

Silver Lion told me that it was time to go and get back into my room in case anyone knocked on the door. This was so strange how it worked, but if you look up as if you were looking at the celling that is how you get out of the hole. Within seconds I looked up and I was straight back in my room under my bed. I got really excited about this, I couldn't wait to tell Ned, but then something inside me said don't, it will be to risky.

I crawled back out from under the bed, all the excitement made me really tired, the Silver Lion pointed at the board and said 'Look Joe, that's what you are learning tomorrow, I'll be watching you from the training ground in secret.'

All warlocks are to be on the training ground by 8am sharp to learn the transformation spell, this will be an all day class and a new teacher will be taking the class

That sounded fun and interesting, I started to wonder who the new teacher was?

'Right Joe, I'm off, you know where i am if you need me.' he laughed and off he went.

I woke up with a huge bang on the door and my eyes flew open was is it morning already? There was daylight flooding my room and I realised that I must have fallen straight to sleep last night. The door banged again and I jumped out of bed, I put my shoes on and Ned woke up and said 'Do you have to wake me up at this time Joe, what are you doing?'

The loud bang happened again and Ned asked what was going on and what was all the noise about? The banging suddenly stopped and then there was silence. There was another bang and a flash and all the books fell to the floor. I heard a voice through the door 'Sorry about that but I had to make sure you are awake, I am your new teacher Mr Ice and I will see you on the training ground in ten minutes.'

This was going to be strange, another teacher training me, I wondered where all these teachers kept coming from? Was there another place where they all hide out or something as I haven't seen Mr Ice before. The door opened and all the students made their way down to the training ground, I then saw Lara walking too. I decided to catch up with her and find out what was going on as I really missed our time together. I ran towards Lara while shouting her name, it just felt like she didn't want to know me any more. Suddenly Lara turned around and she cast a spell towards me to stop me. She walked up to me and said 'Joe don't you get it now, I've moved on to greater things, tonight I'm helping Lady Malaga and all the people in the towns will know and hear about her, she will be everywhere and a warning will be issued to the human race.'

She cast out again to unfreeze me and by the time I could ask what was she going to do she vanished, she was getting more and more like Lady Malaga. What did she mean that people will know about her? I have to warn them, but how when I was stuck in this place. Oh no I'm late for my training! I ran towards the training ground and I could see a very tall man standing there, wearing long robes with blue patterns on, all of the patterns were like the colour of water and he didn't look happy with me. I started walking very slowly as the look on his face didn't look at all good. I just saw a bright blue light heading towards me and struck the ground right beside me, this made me start to run like hell towards him.

'That's better a bit of fire in your belly.'

He started to laugh, by the sounds of things my new teacher likes to have a bit of fun and he laughs a lot, this wouldn't be as bad as I thought. Let's hope he likes me. Mr Ice tells me that he will be teaching me for a bit now and that I will be in safe hands and will love to learn his way of magic. After a few minutes getting to know my new teacher he was ready to start, he did warn me that the lesson today would be very hard and that we have an extra hour for lunch before coming back. He also said tonight the doors to our room would be open a lot longer, as Lady Malaga had said to all the teachers that we must gather on the training ground and find another apprentice to pair up and start battling against each other. Don't worry the teachers will all be there, keeping a close eye on all of us so no one will come to any harm. This sounds like Lady Malaga wants us to be distracted with what I already know. We must put our magic to the test with each other to show the teachers what we have learnt and we will be scored which will show how well we are doing for Lady Malaga. I think this is so she knows who is doing really well and proving their abilities, I'm taking it the losers will be banished to the ends of the world.

I stared at Mr Ice and watched him cast and turn himself into a rock and then a lamp shade. Each time just seeing his kind eyes and big grin on the objects was was making me laugh, then he turned himself back into himself.

'You see Joe, this spell is not easy to learn it but I will say that once you have cracked it you can be anything you want. I must warn you though, each transformation spell you do, it will only last ten minutes, enough time for you to hide from your opponent. They say the more powerful you are, the longer you can transform.

I spent half the morning doing this one spell and all that was happening was a little bit of smoke coming from the ring, Mr Ice was so calm with me and tells me no-one ever gets it on their first attempt apart from Lady Malaga, she is one true powerful Warlock. She had turned so evil, no one has dared to stand up to her or even say anything back to her.

I kept on trying the spell and the more I tried the weaker I got and could barely lift up my hand to cast, it was just like a heavy weight pulling my arm down. Mr Ice did not let me stop up until the point that, I was on the floor with exhaustion and I was just hoping that it was our lunch break. He asked me to cast out again and I'm not sure if I made the cast as all I could see was black as my eye lids shut.

My eyes were so heavy and I could hardly open them, I heard Mr Ice say 'Get up, don't give up.'

I had no more energy to do anything, Mr Ice wasn't having any of it. I heard him cast out, there was a big bang and flash right next to me again, it made me jump and my eyes whipped open, I looked up and saw Mr Ice laughing.

'That will be enough now I can see you have tried your best, when you feel up to it you can go to lunch.'

This was strange as five minutes went by and I was full of beans, I stood right up and started to walk to the hall where all the other apprentices were going for lunch. As I was walking over there, I overheard about the dark gardens, something was going on there and one of the students found out and tried to see what was happening. There was a rumour that they didn't even make it past the first set of trees that were guarding the gardens, some say the trees were really nasty to anyone that dared enter without the say so from Lady Malaga. This was on my mind now, I thought about using the hole to sneak around to see what was going on. Then suddenly it made sense with what was being said as Lara told me something was going to happen. I have Ned telling me that I should check it out and if there is something going on we need to warn the other Warlocks. I grabbed my food and took a seat, I could see another warlock opposite me looking very sad and on his own, I thought I needed to make friends now and I could try and cheer him up. I kept on looking to see if anyone was going to sit next to him, some just looked at him then laughed and this didn't make things any easier for him. I took my food which was chicken soup with bread it was ok but the chunky bits were hard to swallow. I walked over and he raised his head to look at me and then lowered it back down and I spoke out to him. 'My name is Joe, is it ok to seat here?'

He nodded his head to say yes and looked very surprised that someone wanted to sit next to him, I then asked 'Whats your name then?'

He replied 'Patrick but I always get called fat pat.'

He looked so upset that he gets called that name, I made him laugh by saying 'Don't worry I get called Joe with no brains, as people just think that because I'm quiet and don't talk much to others that I'm thick and can't do anything!'

We chatted for some time and I found out a lot about Patrick, he also knew of Lara. She would stick up for him a lot if anyone started on him, he was halfway through his Warlock training, a few times he nearly got cast out. He always showed how hard he was willing to work, I guessed all the students here were on a time frame and if you were no good, you just got cast out to the ends of the world by Lady Malaga. The teachers she had chosen herself to get the job done. He also said he was worried once Lady Malaga has done what she wanted to do, what would happen to us and the people in the world that she can't stand?

Some of the teachers have stood up to her but haven't won, she was just too powerful. Patrick also said that everyone had been waiting for someone special to come along and save them from this dark evil curse. The Warlocks have prayed for years and years but nothing has happened yet. I didn't want to say to him that the person they have been waiting for is me. I couldn't even cast the transformation spell, how was I going to save all the Warlocks and the human race?

We chatted more and finished up our lunch, Patrick was so pleased with himself that he had learnt a new spell and really wanted to show me. He couldn't wait to get outside and show me, but he couldn't be seen doing this spell when not training as this was the rule. Anyone caught doing spells out of hours that was not asked to by any teacher was punished by sending them to Lady Malaga and she would decide what to do, some had a blind eye turned to them but others not so.

Chapter 17

BEST FRIENDS

Patrick and I found a quiet spot behind the hall, Patrick was so happy I've never seen him so happy, it was such a difference to how I just saw him at lunch looking so sad and down, just me walking over had changed the way he was and the smile he had was so enchanting it could make anyone smile. He said to me 'Right Joe are you ready to see this?'

I couldn't wait to see what he had learnt and how happy he was to show me. He cast out and there were bright colours coming out of his ring. There were yellows, reds, blues, pinks and even some purple, all these colours mixed together and I started to see a shape forming. I started to see two legs appear then another two followed by a body then a head. It was so lovely and this all came together and it was a bright colourful horse. Patrick said it was a magic horse that could talk and take you anywhere without being seen. Once you jumped on the back of the horse you are invisible just like the horse, the spell he learnt was out of an old spell book that he found, it was found out in the grounds and he couldn't go into much detail as he didn't want to get anyone in trouble.

I just stared at this beautiful coloured horse and it was like a rainbow that was in the sky this made me so happy with a little tear in my eye as it reminded me of back at home. I used to walk past some fields that had beautiful horses in.

'Beautiful isn't she, you can't tell anyone about this, I have to hide the spell book somewhere.'

Patrick spoke out so quickly and worried that people would see this beautiful horse, he cast out another spell so quickly the horse vanished. He was very quick off the mark with his spells, I did want to tell Patrick I could hide the book for him but I couldn't risk telling him about the secret hiding place, well not just yet. It was nearly time that our lunch is over and we all have to go back to meet our teachers on the training ground, but before we both went we said we will be really good friends and we can meet here at lunch and show each other some of our magic we have learnt helping each other out.

I walked up to the training ground and Mr Ice is there waiting with the grin on his face, he shouts at me. 'Ready to learn the spell again Joe? This time try not to fall on the ground!'

I took my hand and cast again, this time it felt different there was a warm sense of feeling running though my fingers, Mr Ice says 'Yes Joe that's it, don't loose it now concentrate.'

I try with all my might, my hands seem to tighten and the ring started to cast out a yellow smoke, Mr Ice shouts out 'Yes now think of any object you want to turn yourself into Joe.'

I was thinking hard and all I could think of was the horse I saw. I tried to get it out of my mind but I just couldn't. I looked down and my body starts to change into the horse, I could see Mr Ice looking very confused and not looking happy at all, he cast out at me and stopped me from fully casting myself into the horse. I felt a power of force push into me and there was a fight between my cast and Mr Ice, without a doubt Mr Ice's magic over took mine, it was a force that pushed me so hard and fell onto the ground.

Mr Ice walks over to me looking very angry and this was the only time I had seen him not laughing 'Now, where have you seen this Joe? To transform yourself into a horse is very rare and that is magic I saw many years ago. Funny how that book also vanished, have you got something to say Joe?'

I didn't mean to cast myself into a horse, I just couldn't get that out of my head, the bright colours and everything, I didn't know what to say to Mr Ice other than having a dream about it the other night. It might come from there. Mr Ice called the end of the lesson and told me to go back to my room and wait there for him.

Within seconds Mr Ice cast out a spell that made him vanish. I headed back to my room thinking about what I had done, I was now thinking of Patrick and where he is. I needed to tell him. Then in a split second the board on my wall started to smoke I thought it was on fire with the amount of smoke coming from it. It then started to clear and there was writing that appeared.

There has been a report that the book of Warlocks true power and love has been used, this is forbidden, all students will remain in their rooms until their rooms have been searched and signed off. Anyone that does not follow these rules will be punished, the doors will open immediately.

There has been a breach of the Warlock rules. I needed to get to Patrick quick, I didn't know where his room was, how would I leave now as someone will be entering my room anytime now? What was I going to do? My hands were shaking. I didn't want Patrick to get into trouble, if anything I would have the spell book as I know Lady Malaga won't do anything to me as she needs me too much.

Think Joe think. There was movement under my bed and it was Silver Lion, he said he's got a really good idea but I will only have about five minutes to make this work, he says follow me. So I did still shaking we went through the hole, past all the signs until we were at a sign saying rooms, Silver Lion opened the door, and there was a line of all the rooms but only one would be Patricks, Silver Lion said 'Now Joe, use your magic quick and fast, you know which one is his room, I can give you an invisible spell so you can quickly enter into his room without him knowing and grab the book and be back in your room before anyone knows, the only thing is you won't have time to hide it in your hiding place, you will have to take the wrap for your friend Patrick, the choice is yours and make it quick!'

All I was thinking was how nice Patrick was to me and how much of a shame it was that people pick on him, I can't let him take the blame for this, I would call Patrick a really good friend of mine and I've only known him a few days, but that's what friends do, look out for each other. I made the decision to do this, Silver Lion cast out a spell that turned me invisible, I knew what door was Patrick's straight away. I had a good feeling, I walked into his room and the book was there lying on the floor, Patrick was walking up and down pacing, panicking, Silver Lion followed me into the room and said 'Don't worry I will cast a spell on Patrick now to fall asleep, he won't see the book has gone.'

Silver Lion cast the spell and he fell asleep standing up, it was my chance to grab the book. I grabbed it and walked out and then me and silver lion looked up and we were back in my room, but silver lion ran back under the bed just in time as a teacher entered my room.

There I was standing up clutching the book in my hands. The teacher spoke out, she was a different teacher and one I had not seen before, she had orange fizzy curly hair, glasses and a big nose with a squeaky voice. She cast out a spell it was almost like a round mirror appeared in the air, she spoke out and said to the mirror find the book it's here. All of a sudden I saw Lady Malaga's face appear in a cloud of smoke in the mirror. She turns her head in the mirror and says 'Well done, throw the book to me now, and make sure you cast the rat to the Warlock jail I will deal with this later.'

She went but the smoke was still there, the smoke turned into a pair of hands which were pure black, the teacher snatched the book and threw it towards the hands, which grabbed the book and vanished.

The teacher turned to me and before I could say anything she cast straight at me and I was gone from my room.

Everything just melted away and I was pulled through a tunnel that was spinning around, I couldn't see anything apart from the walls around me. There was some writing on some of it but I couldn't make out what it said, I just wanted it to stop, it was giving me such a headache. I had to close my eyes wishing it would stop.

'Welcome to the Warlock jail'

A voice said out loud. I opened my eyes and I wasn't in the tunnel anymore, I was in a dark grey room with rat droppings on the floor, the bars holding me inside were all rusted. A very large guy walked up to the jail holding a scroll he spoke out. 'Joe I see you have been sentenced to the Warlock jail for a breach of the Warlock rules in the Headquarters.'

He kept on reading, but all I could see was a large man, with a funny shaped head that didn't quite fit his body. His eyes were red and a few strands of hair left on his head. He banged the bars with his stick that looked like a walking stick and shouted out. 'You listening to me or day dreaming, you will remain here until I have further notice about what I need to do with you next, it says here that you are a very important case for Lady Malaga.'

My heart skipped a beat, there was something about that name and when it was mentioned it just sent shivers down my spine. I just nodded at the guy as I didn't want to even ask his name, he looked so scary. After he read the scroll he made his way back to a wooden stool and sat down and started to tap his stick on the ground next to him. What I saw next I couldn't believe. A cloud of smoke appeared and a full length table was there with a full banquet. There was chicken, beef, potatoes and vegetables, everything you can imagine having on a roast dinner, he just sat there eating the lot, throwing the bones through the bars at me for my dinner laughing each time saying 'There you go, eat your dinner animal.'

I couldn't believe he just made all this food and had eaten the lot, no wonder he was so big. I saw him pick up the last of the chicken legs, scoff it down and then throw the bones into my cell. He tapped his stick again and this time there were mugs and mugs of beer, after all the excitement of him eating and drinking he fell asleep on the stool, any sound and he would wake up suddenly.

I just sat on the cold wet floor wishing I could go home. Thinking about everyone at home I could hear a whisper coming from one of the walls in the cell, I got up quietly as I didn't want to wake the guard up. I found out where the voice was coming from and walked up to the wall closer and pressed my ear against the wall. It was all old bricks that had been chipped away, it looked like some of them had been clawed at. The brick started to move, I pulled my head back and took the brick out of the wall. I did this so quietly and placed it on the floor, I looked into the wall and I could see a familiar face, I looked more closely and it was Patrick, I couldn't believe his face was inside the wall and he spoke out to me.

'Joe, sorry that you have landed in jail, everyone is talking about it, they are not sure what is going to happen to you and me. I learnt this spell to contact people, so don't be scared Joe I will help you, I know there is a big guy there. Everyone knows him I'm sure he is called Skerge, but listen, my spell will only work for a second, so once my face disappears, I'm going to leave you a bottle behind, use this to escape. I've got to go Joe, the spell is wearing off, you know what to do.'

Patrick left and like he said, there was a bottle left behind with a scroll attached to the bottle it said.

'Use me well, use me good, say the wrong words and you'll end in the dark woods!'

I picked up the bottle and as I did I could hear movement, I almost dropped the bottle on the floor, I turned around and the guard was still asleep but had moved into a different position. I sat back down on the wet floor just looking at the bottle. I thought there must be something else to this, holding it up I looked around the bottom, there was some wording engraved. I held it up to the light and some words started to appear on the wall.

'Save me now help me now.'

I spoke the words out very softly and the bottle started to shake quite rapidly, I had trouble holding on to it. I let it go but the bottle did not fall to the ground, it was floating in the air. The top of the bottle lid was like a cork you would get in a wine bottle, it flew off the top of the bottle and out came the most beautiful pink and blue smoke. I thought this would wake up the guard but the cell was already covered this reminded me of the horse Patrick had summoned. I was starting to panic as there was just so much smoke and it was leaking through the bars towards to the sleepy guard. At one point it looked like he snorted some up his nose, In the cloud of smoke a door appeared. I could hear the guard waking up. I reached for the handle and opened the door, I could just about hear the guard shouting reaching for his keys to open the cell but it was too late I had made it.

Time had frozen, the guard reaching for his keys, upon entering the door I could hear a voice, I turned around and there was my Mum and Dad standing in the cell. They were not their usual selves but almost like a shadow of themselves. Dad spoke out to me, 'You have to be strong and brave and you have to enter through the door.'

Mum also speaks out, 'Joe my darling you are entering a part of your life where you will become a man, we're so proud of you.'

Just by seeing my parents, I fell to the floor feeling so scared and worried. Where will I be heading? Mum floated towards me and so did Dad but their shadows were fading out. Mum says to me I will be going to a place where Lady Malaga wouldn't be able to get me for at least ten years and that I will be safe. They agreed they would come to me through dreams and letters. After they said their goodbyes they faded away. I picked myself back up with my head held high, and I knew I was ready for the next part of my adventure. I walked through the door and the cloud of smoke followed me. The door slammed shut behind me which made me jump a little. I carried on walking through the smoke and couldn't see anything in front of me. I started to see a bright colour coming through the smoke and there it was, it took my breath away, the most eye catching beautifully bright rainbow coloured tree. I knew I would love this part of my journey and I couldn't wait for it to begin.

About the Author

M.S.Rowley was born and raised on the Devonian coastline in the sunny seaside town of Exmouth. This story has been trapped in Martins head ever since Martin could use his imagination. He would spend many days playing and daydreaming about magic. As a child he was obsessed with slight of hand magic tricks and creating worlds filled with all things magical. As a full time business owner and hairdresser, Martin spends his days making people look and feel good with his hair creations. During the world wide pandemic and the following lock down, Martin's fingers found another way to keep busy and started to hit those keys on his MacBook to bring this story to life.

Printed in Great Britain
by Amazon